TAKE FOUR

TAKE FOUR

C.J. SHANE

Published by Rope's End Publishing

ISBN paperback: 978-1-951524-23-4

ISBN e-book: 978-1-951524-24-1

Typesetting services by BOOKOW.COM

Acknowledgments

Sincere thanks go to Tucson graphic designer Lynne East-Itkin for the book cover design, and to Dawn Lewis of County Durham, England, for editorial services.

Letty Valdez Mysteries

Desert Jade 2017

Dragon's Revenge 2018

Daemon Waters 2019

Direct Evidence 2022

Cat Miranda Mysteries

Kissed 2020

Fair Play 2021

The Broken Pot 2022

Iron Horse Mysteries

Take Four 2023

Shadow Man 2023

In the Slips 2024

Clouds 2024

A Closer Look 2024

Contents

1 Sunday Morning

"Hello."

Logan Reid looked up from his notebook and turned toward the sound of a voice nearby. He removed his wire-rim reading glasses and brushed back a wayward strand of hair. There was a young woman standing about six feet away. She was looking at him, a smile on her face.

"Hi," Logan said. He closed his notebook and gestured to a nearby lawn chair. "Have a seat."

"Thanks. My friend Nina told me there's going to be an apartment available here soon. I knocked on the manager's door. It's 1-A, right? But there was no answer." She sat down.

Logan nodded. Blonde hair in a pony tail. Nice smile. Very pretty. He sighed.

"I hope I can rent the apartment. Nina tells me this is a good place to live. Do you know the manager? He? Or she? Nina just said 'Logan.' That could be a guy or a girl, right?"

"Guy. A man, I mean."

"What's he like?"

"He's a grump. He's totally grumpy." Logan smiled.

"Oh, gosh. I hope I can charm him. I'd really like to live here."

Logan didn't know what to say to that.

"Hey, Logan. I see you've already met Zoey." Nina Perry smiled as she came down the backdoor steps of their two-story apartment building known locally as Casa Pacifica.

Zoey Corban turned to look at Logan, eyebrows raised. A smile grew on her face.

Logan shook his head. "Sorry. I was trying to be funny. I guess that didn't work."

Zoey's smile had become a grin. "Nice to meet you."

Nina plopped down in a nearby chair.

Zoey turned to Nina. "Is Logan grumpy? He seems to think he is."

Nina brushed her dark hair away from her eyes. "Nah. He's not really grumpy exactly. He can be stern, though."

"Stern? When am I ever stern?" Logan was surprised to be described that way.

Nina turned to Zoey. "He's the manager, and he has to enforce the rules. Usually that's not a problem, except for those two in apartment 1-C. I mean those losers who just moved out. Thank god. They were so totally obnoxious." She gestured to one of the windows behind her. "That's the one you want to look at, Zoey. Don't worry about Logan. He's a sweetie."

Now Logan was almost embarrassed. "Okay, enough of that, Nina. I'm not a sweetie."

Nina laughed. "Whatever."

Logan turned to Zoey and asked, "Do you want to see the apartment? And what's your name again?"

"My name is Zoey Corban, and yes, I want to see the apartment but later today. I have to go to practice now. Actually I'm here to get an appointment. How about this afternoon? Maybe around half past four?"

"Sure. I'll either be out here or in my apartment. I'll answer the door, and I promise I won't be grumpy."

Zoey grinned. "Okay. See you then." She rose from the chair, gave Nina a quick hug, and said, "Thanks, Nina. See you later." Zoey waved goodbye and took off at a brisk walk down the street.

"How do you know Zoey? Where's she going? What practice?" Logan asked.

"We met and hit it off when I did a music gig at her school. Zoey is coaching a soccer team. The team is having practice this afternoon at Tucson High."

"An athlete, huh? And what about you? What are you doing up so early?"

Nina chuckled. "You must the only person in Tucson who thinks that eleven in the morning is early."

"That's because you're the only musician I know, and since musicians apparently like to play all night, sleeping late doesn't seem unreasonable."

"Not quite all night last night, but almost. The club closed at one in the morning, but there were some out-of-town musicians here for the jazz festival. The guys in my group and I decided to invite them to jam with us. I didn't get home until half past three."

"No wonder you slept late."

"What are you working on? Looks like you're writing." Nina moved to the chair vacated by Zoey.

"Not writing. I'm just making some notes about my dissertation and writing some other stuff, too."

"Your dissertation? I thought you finished that."

"Yes, I did, and I turned it in. It's being reviewed by the committee now." Logan frowned. "My professor is pretty positive about it. He thinks I should write a book based on the dissertation. So I'm making notes about what I'd have to do to turn it into something readable, not dry, boring academic bullshit, and then I have to figure out which publisher to approach. Not very exciting."

"You don't look very happy." Nina's tone was sympathetic.

"It's just more work. I'm kind of tired of this academic stuff. I've been in school too long, and I've been working on the dissertation for too long."

"If you could do anything else, I mean if you could do what you really want to do, what would that be?"

Logan frowned again, thoughtful this time. "I really don't know. Maybe take a road trip with Charlie. He's never seen the ocean. We could go to California or to Mexico and see the Sea of Cortez or the Pacific."

"How is Charlie?"

"He's doing great. He loves kindergarten, and he loves his teacher. Right now he's doing his regular overnighter with one of his classmates. The kid's name is Javier, but everyone calls him Javie. His mom and I worked out a deal. She has to work on Saturdays so I pick up Charlie and Javie from school Friday afternoon. They spend the night here, and Javie stays for Saturday during the day. Then they go to Javie's house for Saturday night and most of Sunday. Today is Sunday so Maria will bring him back late this afternoon. Javie's family is Mexican American so Charlie gets some really good meals there. Javie's grandmother is a terrific cook."

"So that gives you Saturday night to go out and party." Nina grinned.

Logan rolled his eyes. "I'm too boring to be partying. So how did this late-night jam go? Meet anyone interesting?"

"The jam was really great. There was a sax player, this cat from New York City who couldn't stop talking about how he likes the food in Tucson. He went on and on about *chimichangas*. Apparently he'd never eaten one before."

Logan nodded. "He's not the first to enjoy the Sonoran cuisine here. Did he stop talking about food long enough to play?"

"Yeah, he was good, too. They were all good. A guitarist was there and another pianist – I gave up my keyboard to her for a couple of tunes. Oh yeah, a bassist, too, really good. My bassist Vic bowed out, and this cat from LA took over."

"I find it amusing that you refer to them as 'cats.'"

"Typical jazz lingo." Nina grinned. "Gotta keep the jazz traditions alive."

"Will there be another late night session tonight?"

"Nah. Usually the club closes up earlier because there are never as many customers on Sunday night. Too many of us have jobs to go to on Monday for us to stay up really late. I'm giving a music lesson late tomorrow morning, and in the afternoon, I do my gig at the bookstore. My boss moved me to the music section so I'm mainly handling CDs and some old LPs and sheet music, not books."

Nina pushed her soft dark curls away from her face and frowned. "My manager said he'd like to give me a pay raise since I know more about music than the average person working for him. But he claims he can't. The owner of the bookstore said no to any pay raises. Obviously, the owner is not into fair wages or rewarding employees who actually know something. Like, take my case. I know a lot about music, and I can talk to the customers and answer their questions." She shrugged her shoulders. "But it is what it is. No pay raise." Nina paused and sighed. "What about you? Other than your struggle sessions with maybe writing a book, what are you up to these days?"

"Same old same old. I'm on semester break now, but, in a couple of weeks, I'll go back to work as a teaching assistant. If my dissertation is approved, and I think it will be, I'll earn my doctoral degree. Graduation is in May. Right now I should be looking for a full-time job for next fall. But I don't want to do that."

"No? You'd get paid a lot more if you were a full-time professor."

"True. But Charlie and I would have to move. Leave Tucson, I mean. We'd have to go to some university town god knows where. Maybe someplace in a cold climate." He shuddered. "But it's more than the climate. I had to move around a lot as a kid because my dad was in the military so Tucson is the only real home I've ever known. I like it here, and I don't want to leave. Plus all the change would be hard on Charlie. New school. Making new friends. All that."

"Well, then you'll have to come up with some way of making a living here like the rest of us."

Logan nodded. "I'm thinking about it. I have a special page in this notebook titled 'How to Make a Living.' Want to hear my ideas?"

"Sure."

Logan opened his notebook. "Okay. First, I'll keep my job here as apartment manager. That means my rent will be reduced by quite a bit. We won't have to move, and Charlie will still be close to his school. Next, maybe turn my dissertation into a crime thriller with a lot of hot sex and make a gazillion dollars?" He looked up at Nina and wiggled his eyebrows.

"You know what the problem with that is, don't you?" Nina grinned.

"What?"

"You're not getting any hot sex. You need to get laid before you write that book." Nina wiggled her eyebrows right back at him.

"Hmmm… whatever." Logan frowned.

"Yeah, whatever. Keep going." She gestured to Logan's notebook.

"Okay, here's more ideas. Maybe a gig as an adjunct prof at our community college. Maybe they'd hire me to teach at least two classes. A full-time prof is not really an option since students don't exactly stand in line to sign up for a philosophy class. Not a lot of demand. Next, free-lance writer on a bunch of different topics. I have some ideas for that. Next, ESL teacher. I actually have some experience with tutoring Japanese students who were learning English when my dad was stationed in Japan. Bookstore clerk. Or maybe I could be a jazz musician." He looked at her and smiled.

Nina laughed. "Good one. But, the last I heard, you don't play an instrument. And I've never heard you sing."

Logan shrugged his shoulders. "Well, there is that. Here's another one. Full-time gardener. Grow vegetables and sell them at the farmer's market."

"I bet you'd like that. You spend a fair amount of time in our community garden anyway." Nina gestured toward where the Iron Horse Community Garden was located a couple of blocks to the south.

"I would like doing that, but I doubt that would make much money. Most people aren't especially interested paying for homegrown Chinese cabbage or okra."

"I think you'd like working in a bookstore. I'll let you know if there's an opening where I work. We could gang up on the manager and demand a pay raise. Or we could get Frida to have a talk with them. She's good at getting pay raises for workers. Meanwhile, how about a job as a dog walker?"

"What? People get paid to walk dogs?" Logan looked skeptical.

"Sure! A lot of folks these days work long hours all week. They hire a walker to come in, take the dog out

7

for a long walk, and then take the dog back home. If you choose weekday mornings, you'll be free when Charlie is home."

"I like dogs." Logan opened his notebook and scribbled a few words.

"Of course, you'll piss off your cat if you come home smelling like a dog." Nina looked over at a scruffy tabby cat lying on the apartment building's side door steps. The cat's front paws were folded under his chest and his golden eyes were half-closed.

"He's not my cat. He just sort of showed up and adopted us."

"You feed him, you got him his vaccinations shots, and you gave him a name, so he's yours," Nina chuckled. "As I remember, his name is Shevek. What does that word mean anyway?"

"Shevek was the main character a sci-fi novel called *The Dispossessed*. Excellent novel."

"Why did you name the cat after that character?"

"Shevek is a theoretical physicist, and his home planet is an anarchist socialist society. He's his own man and doesn't really follow rules. He doesn't exactly fit in any-where. Shevek the Cat is like that. He never comes when I call him. He only comes if he thinks he'll get something to eat."

Nina nodded. "Well, don't give up finding a way to make a living so you can stay here in Tucson. I'd miss you and Charlie terribly if you moved away. You'll think of something. But try to come up with something that doesn't take all your time. Charlie needs you, especially since he doesn't have a mom anymore."

Logan nodded.

Nina looked behind her at their apartment building.

"Any news from my fellow tenants?"

"I'm waiting for Marc to call. He's back East doing one of his photojournalism gigs, but he's coming home in a few days. He told me he was calling from some airport somewhere to ask me if it would be okay to bring home a dog. He's supposed to call again around mid-day today. But you know Marc. He's often late so he may not call until noon or even this afternoon. Or tomorrow. Or next week." Logan shrugged.

"And since you're our apartment manager, you have to give permission for the dog?"

"Exactly. I told him yes. Charlie and I have Shevek, and Frida has a new cat in her apartment, too. It's just a kitten. I think she named it Bonita. So we might as well have a dog, too. I gave Marc the owner's list of rules that pet owners have to follow, and he has to put down a pet deposit. He agreed. He said he has a story to tell us about the dog. I hope the dog wasn't abused. I hate it when animals are mistreated."

"Me, too. We have seven apartments in Casa Pacifica so I'm surprised there are only two of us with pets. You and Frida. Marc will make three. I'd like to have a pet. Maybe I'll get a goldfish."

Logan chuckled. "Yeah, goldfish are so lovable."

"I wouldn't be good for a dog. My schedule is too irregular. Dogs need to go out and do their thing earlier than eleven in the morning. I had a cat for years when I was growing up, and he liked to sit on my face when I was trying to sleep. That wouldn't work either. I don't get enough sleep as it is. A goldfish might be all right."

"Okay. Well, I guess that makes sense. Sort of." Logan paused. "Do you think Zoey will fit in well with the rest of us?"

"Yes, definitely. She'll very likely become a member of our group. Other than those weirdos who are moving out, the rest of us already here have grown close. We're tenants, but we're also kind of a peculiar little family, and it's kind of like you're the big brother."

Logan chuckled. "Big brother, huh? Well, I'm glad you didn't say 'daddy.'"

The two friends sat together in companionable silence in the January sun as they watched people walk by on the sidewalk in front of their apartment building.

Nina spoke first. "I'm starving. Vic told me to come by the store this morning. He has some new Chinese fast food thing he thinks I'll like. He said I can heat it up in the microwave oven."

"Sounds wonderful." Logan made a face.

Nina stood up. "Want to come along? It's a nice day for a walk."

"Sure. I could use a walk. Wait a minute, and I'll get some money in case I see anything I want. Not frozen, microwaved, Chinese fast food, though." Logan gathered his notebook and pen, and disappeared for a few minutes. He returned quickly. "Okay. I'm ready."

The two headed east, walking at a leisurely pace.

"I don't know how Vic does it," Logan said. "He's married, he's got two kids, he's the assistant manager of the Fast-In-Out store, and he's your band's bassist. Does he ever sleep?"

"Probably not," Nina answered. "He never complains either. I hope Vic will always have time for music because he's really a terrific bassist. Reminds me of Ron Carter."

About ten minutes later, they pushed open the glass door to the Fast-In-Out quick stop store.

"Hey, Vic," Nina called out.

The tall, thin, black man behind the counter grinned when he saw them. "Hello. How are you today? Miss Nina, Mr. Logan, nice to see you both."

Logan waved. "Mr. Vic, good to see you, too. I wonder if you have any more of the Ghirardelli chocolate."

"So," Vic smiled, "you're a Ghirardelli fan?"

"It's exquisite. My only fear is addiction."

"That's definitely something to fear. Take a look over there in the candy section. And, Nina, the Chinese dish is in the freezer just across from the chocolate. The microwave is here behind the counter. Indulge yourself."

Logan and Nina made their way to the row with the goodies they were seeking. Nina quickly located the frozen dish and came to stand next to Logan in the candy section. They both bent over and peered at the items on a lower shelf.

"Look at that," Logan breathed out. "Something new. White chocolate swirled with dark chocolate."

"Yum. I may have to try that," Nina said.

Suddenly there was a loud crashing noise at the front of the store. Logan and Nina stood up to see what had caused the racket. They could see a man dressed in black with a black knit cap and black mask on his face standing at the open door. He stepped forward, and the door closed behind him. At the same time, he pulled a gun out and pointed it at Vic.

"Not good," Logan whispered. He crouched down and pulled Nina down next to him. He and Nina both peered around the end of the row of merchandise. They could see that the man with the gun had all his attention on Vic. Logan reached for his cell phone. He pressed 9-1-1 and whispered into the phone.

2 ONE DOWN

"Don't move!" the man yelled. "Hands up!"

Vic's hands crept upward. "I'm not moving. What do you want?"

The man laughed roughly. "I'm here to put you out of business." He tightened his grip on the gun. He laughed again, then he yelled loudly as he pulled the trigger, "One down!"

The bullet slammed into Vic's midsection. He fell backwards, blood streaming from the gunshot wound in his lower chest.

Nina gasped. She stood up and cried out. "No!"

The gunman turned toward the sound of Nina's voice. Logan was standing next to her now, pulling her back with one hand, his other hand holding his cell phone. Now the barrel of the gun was pointed directly at Nina and Logan.

Just at that moment, the outer door swung open again. Another customer stepped into the store. A man. Tall, dark hair, wearing khaki pants with his long-sleeve dress shirt rolled up to the elbows, a tie loose around his neck, and a briefcase in one hand. He took one look at the man with the gun and froze.

The gunman turned toward the sound of the door opening. He flashed the gun at the new customer, and with his other hand, he shoved the man out of the way. He fled the store at a run.

Both Logan and Nina ran to Vic. Blood was steadily seeping out of a hole in Vic's chest, and he was groaning in pain. Logan handed his phone to Nina.

"Call 9-1-1 again and tell them we need an ambulance." Nina complied, struggling to control her trembling voice as tears began to roll down her cheeks.

Logan looked around, found a roll of paper towels and ripped it open. He quickly folded the towels into a thick square-shaped pad. He pulled Vic's shirt open and pressed the paper towel pad against the wound. By this time, Vic had slumped down and was lying flat on his back, Logan kneeling over him and pressing on the makeshift tourniquet.

"Stay with me, Vic. Help is coming," Logan said in a low voice.

The man who had entered the store a moment before came around the front desk and squatted near Logan. "Can I help?"

"See if you can find any gauze so I can make a better tourniquet. These paper towels are not all that great. There's a first-aid section in the row on the left."

The man nodded and went quickly to the first-aid supplies. He returned with two rolls of gauze, ripping open one package as he came.

"Thanks," Logan said. He removed the blood-soaked paper towels and took the first roll of gauze. He pressed it against the wound.

"Is he breathing?" the man asked.

"Oh, shit. No!"

"I know CPR," the dark-haired man said. "Here, you continue to press with the tourniquet, and I'll try to get his heart going again. I think the shock of the wound caused his heart to freeze up." He moved to kneel over Vic's prone body, and he quickly began the CPR chest compressions.

Logan watched the rhythmic flexing of the muscles in the man's brown arms and hands. He could hear the man counting under his breath as he pressed on Vic's chest. Logan continued to apply pressure to the wound, but now, the bleeding appeared to have reduced to a trickle.

"I'm Logan. I'm glad you're here," he said to the stranger.

The man paused for a few seconds. "My name is Gwilym. And I'm glad you're here, too." He returned to the chest compressions.

Nina spoke, still struggling with tears. "I hear sirens."

"Good!" both Logan and Gwilym muttered.

"I'm going to the door and wave them in," Nina said.

"Before you go out, make sure that asshole with the gun isn't there," Logan growled.

Nina went to the door and peeked out. "He's gone. I see the ambulance coming." She went out and began waving to the ambulance. Two police cars were behind the ambulance.

"He's breathing again," Logan said. "I think you can stop the CPR."

Gwilym nodded and moved away from Vic's torso.

Two EMTs with a stretcher came into the store. Logan stood and pointed to Vic. The EMTs knelt beside him. They quickly examined the wounded man.

One of them looked up at Logan. "Looks good. You got the bleeding pretty much stopped. I think we can move him now."

"You should know Vic stopped breathing. He got Vic's heart going again." Logan gestured to Gwilym who had stepped back and out of the way.

The two EMTs brought the stretcher around behind the counter, carefully placed Vic on it, and they strapped him in. It only took them a couple of minutes to move him to the back of the ambulance. One of the EMTs stayed with

Vic, and the other drove off toward the nearest hospital, sirens blaring.

Two cops had already entered the store.

"What happened here?" One of police officers was looking directly at Logan.

"Nina and I came for something to eat. While we were here, this guy came in with a gun and shot Vic."

Nina stifled a sob. "His name, I mean the one who got shot, his name is Vic Davis. He's in my group."

"What group?" The policeman asking the questions had a notebook and was writing in it. The other policeman was behind the counter taking a closer look.

"I have a jazz group. Our name is Take Four. Vic plays the bass." Nina wiped away tears. "I play piano."

"And Vic Davis works here, too?"

"Yes. He's the assistant manager. I need to call his wife."

The policeman turned to Logan. "You are her husband, boyfriend, what?"

"We're friends, but also she and I live in the same apartment building where I'm the manager. We live just a couple of blocks away. I was outside enjoying this sunny day when Nina came downstairs, and we decided to walk down here and get Nina something to eat," Logan said.

"Who are you?" He gestured to Gwilym.

"I'm Gwilym Havard. I'm a Canadian visiting Tucson for the annual jazz festival. I just came in for a cup of coffee."

"Okay, let's see everyone's ID."

Nina and Logan produced Arizona driver's licenses. Gwilym handed the cop his passport.

The cop wrote down license and passport numbers, then returned the documents.

"Okay. I want each of you, one at a time, to tell me what happened. You go first." He gestured to Logan.

"Nina and I were over there behind that row of goods. We were bent down looking at the chocolate. All of a sudden, we heard the front glass door thrown open. It was pushed open so hard that it hit the wall. This guy was already in the store. He pulled out a gun and pointed it at Vic."

Nina began crying in earnest. Logan handed her a paper towel.

"Describe the man," the cop said.

"He was dressed in black clothes, and he had a black knit cap and black mask on."

"What did he do?"

"When I saw the gun, I pulled Nina down beside me so the gunman wouldn't see us. I called 911 on my phone. Then the gunman yelled at Vic."

"What did he say?"

"He said, 'I'm here to put you out of business.' Then he yelled really loudly, 'One down!' and he pulled the trigger."

Nina was sobbing by now. Gwilym was standing close to her with a frown on his face. He reached out and patted her shoulder.

The cop looked at Logan and said, "He didn't demand that the cash register be opened? He didn't try to steal money or anything?"

"No," Logan answered. "This all happened really fast. He didn't seem to want anything other than to shoot Vic."

The cop looked at Gwilym. "Anything to add?"

"I'd say the man was about five feet nine or ten inches and fairly slender build. He had on black shoes, light weight boots, I think."

The cop took notes on this.

"When I came into the store, I didn't know this was going on. I just stopped and stared when I saw the man had a gun. I didn't know what to do." Gwilym shook his head.

"Oh, I forgot," Logan said. "Just after he shot Vic, Nina stood up and choked out 'No!' The gunman turned and pointed the gun at us. That's when Gwilym came in the door."

Gwilym added, "The gunman turned toward me, pushed me out of the way, and ran out the door."

The cop turned to Nina. "Anything to add?"

"No, I can't think of anything." She wiped tears from her face.

"Have any of you seen this man before?"

"No," they all said at once.

"And what did he mean when he said 'One down'?"

Logan and Gwilym shook their heads.

Nina began sobbing again. "I don't know. I don't know."

The cop nodded. "Okay, write your names, addresses and contact information in my notebook. I may have to contact you again with more questions."

All three complied.

"Okay, you can leave now. We'll be here for a while."

The three went outside.

Logan turned to Gwilym. "Want to go back to the apartments with us? I can make us some coffee. No. Forget that. We can have a cold beer."

Gwilym nodded. "Good idea. I'll leave my car here." He turned to Nina. "You okay?"

"I guess so." She sighed heavily. "I have to call Vic's wife. She'll be so upset. Maybe I can go visit Vic at the hospital later this evening or tomorrow."

The three began walking side-by-side back toward Logan and Nina's apartment building.

When they arrived, Nina turned to the two men. "I'll be back in a little while. I'm going to go up to my apartment and call Vic's wife and the other guys in our group. And I'm going to cancel my tutoring session and call in sick to work at the bookstore."

"Have a seat, Gwilym," Logan said. "So, you want a beer?"

"Yes. That would be great."

"Back in a minute," Logan said. He disappeared and returned shortly with two cold beers.

"Ah," Gwilym said, tasting the beer. "This is some of that Tucson craft beer. Excellent."

"Yeah, for sure you can get good beer here in Tucson."

"And good food, too. And great jazz. I always enjoy my visits here."

"I'm sorry this happened, Gwilym. You came for the jazz fest and…"

Gwilym nodded. "Oh, well. Shit happens."

Logan nodded. "Ain't that the truth."

They both took another swig from their beer bottles.

After a few minutes of quiet, Gwilym spoke. "When we were walking here to your place, I saw this sign that said Iron Horse Neighborhood. What does that mean? I thought Iron Horse was an old-fashioned way of referring to trains."

"Exactly. Our neighborhood was originally home to the railroad workers when the railroad first came to Tucson. The rail line runs just south of here and in an east-west direction with a station downtown for stops. You can hear it when it passes." Logan gestured to the south. "Our neighborhood isn't all that big. To the north is Tucson High School and the University of Arizona is a bit farther to the northeast. To the east is Euclid Avenue, to the south, there's the rail line and a big parkway that goes to downtown Tucson."

"And that Rattlesnake Bridge," Gwilym smiled. "That's quite impressive. It actually looks like a rattlesnake."

"Yeah, you can bike or hike over the parkway on the Rattlesnake Bridge."

Logan gestured to the apartment building behind him. "This building used to be a big mansion that was owned by one of the railroad execs. He called it Casa Pacifica because they were building the railroad east to Texas and west all the way to California and the Pacific. It was built over one hundred years ago. Someone bought it maybe fifty years ago and converted it into an apartment building. There are three apartments downstairs and a small laundry room and kitchenette. Upstairs there are four apartments."

Gwilym looked at the stuccoed, two-story building in Spanish Revival style with its large arched windows on both floors.

"Casa Pacifica is a terrific name for such a beautiful old building. I really admire the Spanish Revival architecture. I bet the apartments have high ceilings and polished wooden floors."

"Yes, that's a good description."

"And where is the western boundary of your Iron Horse Neighborhood?"

"Fourth Avenue. There's a lot of shops and clubs on Fourth Avenue."

"Yes, I've been there."

The two men fell silent for a while.

"What do you think will happen now?" Gwilym asked.

"Don't know. I hope the cops find that guy and fast. This whole thing is totally weird. I mean the dude didn't even try to steal anything. He went straight for shooting Vic. What's that about?"

Gwilym put his empty bottle on the table in front of them.

"Want another one?" Logan asked.

"No, thanks. Better not. I heard Nina play at the jazz fest, and I heard her again last night at a club on Fourth

Avenue. She's a brilliant jazz musician. She's very beautiful, too. What do you know about her?"

Logan looked at Gwilym and frowned.

"Oh." Gwilym got the message. He was disappointed. "I guess that means you're her boyfriend or husband?"

A brief smile appeared on Logan's face. "No. More like her big brother." He paused then said quietly. "Just so you know, I try to watch out for Nina, and the other tenants, too. Nina is totally into her music. She doesn't pay much attention to what's going on around her, which can be dangerous, especially for a woman. She's way too trusting. And she's had her share of trouble with men."

Gwilym chuckled. "That sounds like a warning."

Logan shrugged. "Just so you know."

"Well, you're not going to be happy to hear this. She walked home last night from the club on Fourth Avenue. A man followed her nearly the entire way."

Logan's frown deepened. "How do you know this?"

"I know it because I was following the man who was following Nina. I was waiting around outside hoping I could meet her and tell her how much I enjoyed her music. That's when I saw this dude lurking nearby. Nina took off down the street, and he was fairly close behind her. She didn't seem to notice him. I didn't want her to get hurt so I followed them both."

"Did this dude look like the one who shot Vic?"

Gwilym shook his head. "I can't say for sure. He was about the same size as the shooter, but it was too dark see much. He stuck to the shadows, and I never saw his face."

"An odd coincidence."

"Yeah, it is," Gwilym replied. "I just wanted Nina to be safe. I mean it when I say she's a real treasure when it comes to the keyboard."

"And beautiful." Logan smiled.

Gwilym chuckled. "Yeah, well, for sure. But I'm serious about her music. I own a jazz club in Vancouver. I have this idea about asking her and her group to do some gigs at my club. I would pay for all expenses. We have a big jazz festival in June. She could escape the Tucson summer heat and come and play for a bunch of enthusiastic Canadian jazz fans."

Logan chuckled. "Okay. So I guess you really are serious about her music."

"Very serious." Gwilym frowned. "Of course, her bassist getting shot changes things. I'm not sure what Nina will do now."

Just at that moment, Nina emerged from the side door of the building. She came and sat at the table with Logan and Gwilym.

"Nina, want a beer?"

"No thanks. I'll just start crying again."

Logan and Gwilym exchanged confused glances, not sure what beer had to do with tears.

Nina sighed. "I called everyone. Vic's wife is on her way to the hospital."

"What about the other guys in your group?" Logan asked.

"Santiago and Zeke are both okay. They were shocked when I told them about Vic."

"What about your group now? What will you do without a bassist?" Gwilym asked.

"I don't know. We have to have Vic. The bass is our foundation. I guess we'll just keep playing, the three of us, until he's better, although the music won't be the same without Vic. We have to play tonight and for a couple more evenings."

"Why is that?" Gwilym asked.

"We signed a contract for the days at the end of the jazz fest and right after. Some people who go to the jazz fest hang around for a few days. They like to go to clubs in the evening and hear more jazz from the local groups. We're here for them."

"That describes me," Gwilym said. "I was there at the club last night. Your group is really fabulous. You in particular. You remind me of Keith Jarrett."

"Oh, gosh. Thanks. That's quite a complement," Nina said. "Keith Jarrett has always been one of my favorites." She sighed.

Logan looked at Gwilym. "Want to tell her what you saw last night?"

Gwilym nodded. "Nina, I was waiting around hoping to talk to you after the last session. I saw you leave the club. but before I could approach you, I saw this guy dressed in dark clothes following you. I couldn't see his face. It was too dark. I decided to follow him because he was following you."

Nina's eyes went wide.

"Once we left Fourth Avenue, the streets got darker. He followed you back here to this apartment building. He watched you unlock the front door and go inside. Then he walked away. I was in the shadows across the street so I'm fairly certain he never saw me."

"And I never saw him. What do you think he wanted?" she asked.

Logan and Gwilym exchanged glances. Both frowned.

"Are you planning on walking home again tonight?" Logan asked.

"Sure. How else would I get home? You know I don't have a car," Nina answered.

Logan looked at Gwilym. "Can you walk her home? I can't leave Charlie."

"Yes, of course. Who's Charlie?"

"My son. He's five years old."

"That okay with you, Nina?" Gwilym asked.

"Definitely," Nina smiled. "You're such a gentleman. Maybe that guy was just a fan."

Logan and Gwilym exchanged glances.

"Maybe," they said at the same time. They were both frowning.

"How about if I come by here this evening and walk you to the club as well as home?" Gwilym asked. "In fact, we could have dinner together. I'd really enjoy talking to you about our favorite music."

Logan's lips twitched trying not to laugh.

Nina smiled and looked a little embarrassed. "That would be lovely."

"Okay. I'll come around six this evening. Be prepared to recommend a restaurant."

"Or you could eat here with the rest of us," Logan said.

"Oh, yes," Nina said. "I didn't think about that. We have sort of a potluck on Sunday evenings. All of us in the apartment building get together. Want to come and eat with us instead of going to a restaurant?"

"That would be very nice. I appreciate the invitation. What should I bring?"

Nina smiled and nodded. "Oh, you don't have to bring anything since you'll be our guest. Come up to my apartment first and help me carry some food down. My apartment is 2-A upstairs, above Logan's apartment. Just go up the front steps into the building. Then when you are inside, go up the stairs to the second floor. My door is right there. I'll see you around six then."

Gwilym stood. "Nice meeting you both, even if it was under some really bad circumstances. I'm going to walk back to the convenience store and get my car. Nina, see you later."

They all said their goodbyes, and Gwilym took off walking down the street.

"Nice guy," Nina said.

"Yeah, he seems like an upright dude. He really helped Vic a lot." Logan looked at her. "Nina, sweetheart, you're such a space case. You need to pay more attention to what's going on around you. It worries me that some stranger was following you home last night." Logan frowned.

"Oh, quit worrying, Logan. If you want to worry, worry about Charlie since you're his daddy. I'll be okay." She stood. "I'm going upstairs now and take a shower and get something for breakfast or lunch. Whatever. Don't forget Zoey is coming later this afternoon to look at the apartment."

Logan nodded and frowned again. "You're a space case."

"Maybe you really are a grump. But I love you anyway." Nina blew him a kiss as she turned and walked back into the apartment building.

3 A NEW TENANT

Gwilym walked away with a light step. He really liked and admired Nina. He thought she was a far better musician than any of the jazz pianists he knew. Listening to her play at the jazz fest, and again last night at the Fourth Avenue club, had been wonderful. Her jazz lines were exquisite: always original, tinged with the flavor of the blues, an intellectual challenge but sensuous at heart. Reminded him of a few days he spent in New Orleans a couple of years back. And her band members were right with her, too. Vic, the bassist, would shift the chords, and Nina stepped in with something original and always rich and even provocative. Occasionally she would play by herself when the others in the group took a break. She was so good. She was good with her group, and she was good alone. No. More than good. "Brilliant" was the right word to use. It had been a long time since he'd been this excited about a jazz musician.

He frowned. Why wasn't she more famous? Better known? She could be, he thought, if she had some help. Someone who knew the business. Someone who made it possible for Nina to focus on her art, to be herself, to play the music of the gods.

Was Gwilym that person? That special someone who could help her?

Or was he fooling himself? Was it really that she was beautiful and sweet? And he wanted nothing more than to hold her close. He had to admit to himself that he was really attracted to her.

Gwilym frowned. He remembered how Nina had reacted when he told her about the man following her last night. Her response had been sweet. Probably a fan, she'd said. Logan's response was quite different. He obviously didn't think that the man was a fan, nor did Gwilym. He decided right then and there that he was going to do whatever it took to keep Nina safe as long as he was here in Tucson, even if that meant extending his visit. He didn't really see that as a problem. He was released from his duties while he worked on his book. Everything at his bookstore back in Vancouver was going as usual. The assistant manager of his club was taking care of everything. He and Gwilym texted each other a couple of times a day. The groups were following the schedule. The patrons were showing up, buying drinks, and enjoying the jazz music. No problems.

So yeah, he said to himself. Gwilym was going to do what he could to keep Nina safe, and hope, hope, hope that he got a chance to know Nina a whole lot better.

By that time, he had returned to the parking lot of the convenience store where Vic had been shot. The police were removing the yellow tape from the scene. The store's lights were off. An older man was locking the front door.

"Hi," Gwilym said. "I'm Gwilym Havard. I was here when that guy with the gun shot the assistant manager."

The man turned to him. "Yeah, the police told me about you. Thank you so much for helping Vic. You and Logan Reid. You two saved Vic's life." He stuck his hand out. "I'm Fred Spier. I own this place."

"Have you heard anything about the shooter? Have the police found him?"

"No. Not the last I heard. He seems to have disappeared into thin air. Looks like Vic will be in the hospital at least for a couple of days or more. I'll be in tomorrow to open up again. I've got a gun under the counter in case the shooter shows up again."

Gwilym frowned. "Okay. Good luck. I hope the best for you all."

He waved goodbye, got into his car, and drove to his hotel room in downtown Tucson. A short nap and a shower would come first, then he'd go buy something for the Casa Pacifica dinner. Maybe two or three bottles of wine. Or some ice cream. Or both. Logan has a kid, Gwilym remembered. The little boy can eat ice cream and the rest of us can drink wine. Yes, a treat for everyone.

A couple of hours later, Gwilym was showered, rested, and almost ready to go, but he was having trouble figuring out what to wear. His hotel bed was covered with rejected clothing. He wanted to look relaxed but cool. Sophisticated, but not intimidating. He wanted most of all for Nina to like what she saw when she looked at him.

"Good grief, Havard," he muttered to himself. He was acting like a teenager getting ready for his first date. "Get over yourself."

He settled on some casual khaki pants and a lightweight, long-sleeved, black knit sweater. On the way out of his hotel room, he grabbed a heavier-weight sweater. Desert nights, especially in January, could get chilly. Or maybe he would have a chance to be a gentleman and drape the sweater over Nina's shoulders.

Gwilym shook his head. "Grow up, Havard."

On his way out of the hotel, he asked the desk clerk for a grocery store recommendation, one that sold wine. She gave him the name of a close-by store and directions on how to find it. About forty-five minutes later, he showed up at Nina's apartment with four bottles of wine and two tubs of ice cream, one chocolate and one pistachio.

~~~

Logan was sitting outside again when Zoey appeared in the late afternoon. He looked up and saw her walking briskly toward him. She waved, smiling, and he returned her wave and smile. He put the lease documents in his briefcase and stood.

"Hi, Logan," she said. "Ready to show me the apartment?"

"Sure. Let me warn you first. The apartment is a mess. There were two guys living here who were already here when I moved in. Supposedly they were both students at the university, but it seemed to me that their main interest was in partying and damaging everything. I had spoken to the owner about evicting them, but they decided to leave on their own. They've only been gone a couple of days. Come with me."

Logan went to the side entrance into the apartment building. "We'll go through the laundry room to the hallway, and then to the apartment door entrance." He went up a few steps, and Zoey followed him. A minute later, they were in the central hall that ran through the building's first floor.

Logan unlocked the apartment door, stepped aside, and let Zoey enter first. She stiffened and muttered, "Oh my god. What a disaster."

There was trash everywhere. They could see a hole in the living room wall where something had smashed against it. Stains of some kind streamed down another wall. The kitchen looked like it hadn't been cleaned in forever. She peeked into the bathroom, turned to Logan with her nose wrinkled, and said, "Yuck. Smells awful."

He nodded. "Needless to say, they lost their deposit."

Zoey went to the bedroom. There were two twin size beds, both with mattresses ripped up.

"All the furniture, including the beds, will be gone this week. Are you okay with renting an unfurnished apartment?"

"I prefer that. I have my own bed and a few other things, including a couple of bookshelves and a rocking chair. It will be fun for me to go to used furniture stores and find anything else I might need."

"You'll be glad to know that I have a team coming in to clean up and repair all this damage. I'll make sure the plumbing and electricity are in good order, too. I should have all this taken care of before the end of this week. You can move in a little early if you wish."

"Lovely." Zoey smiled. "I'm so happy to find this apartment. It's convenient, and Nina raves about the other tenants, including the grumpy manager."

Logan smiled. "I'll try to be nice from now on. Let's go sit outside, and I'll show you the lease."

They returned to sit at the big table on the front lawn. Just at that moment, Shevek the Cat appeared. He jumped onto Zoey's lap, settled down and began to purr. Zoey stroked his head and back.

"Is this your cat?" she asked.

"Sort of. He adopted us."

"What's his name?"

"Shevek."

"Really. From that Ursula Le Guin novel *The Dispossessed*?"

Logan looked at her in surprise. "You know that book?"

"Sure. Ursula Le Guin is one of my favorite authors."

Logan nodded. He reached into his briefcase and pulled out two copies of the lease.

"This is pretty standard. I'll need a rental deposit from you, rent on the first of the month, and you agree to not do any damage to the place and to behave yourself. No wild parties." Logan looked at Zoey. She was smiling again.

"I'll promise to be good," she chuckled. "I don't want to upset the grumpy manager."

Logan made a face, trying not to laugh. He felt a little embarrassed.

"You have a job, and you can pay the rent on time?"

"I'm a teacher at Tucson High."

"Soccer coach?"

"No, that's just a volunteer thing. I teach biology."

"Do you have a roommate or a pet?"

"No and no."

"You have to discuss this with me in advance if you acquire either. We have a pet deposit that's extra."

Zoey nodded. Shevek jumped down from her lap and sauntered off.

"So. Do you want to rent the place?"

"Yes, definitely."

"Okay, take the lease with you. There are two copies. Read it carefully, then sign both copies. You can drop off one copy with a deposit check to me in the next day or two. That's pretty much everything." He sat back in his chair.

Zoey was grinning. "Nina said you all are kind of a family, except for those two who just moved out."

Logan nodded. "You could say that. Nina says I'm the big brother. I don't know what the others think. You can meet us this evening because we're having our regular Sunday evening potluck dinner. One of the residents is not in town, but you can meet everyone else."

"Oh, I wish I could. I have a friend visiting for a few days, and I promised to take her to one of Tucson's famous restaurants. She's kind of a foodie. Maybe next Sunday evening?"

"Sure," Logan said.

Just at that moment, a car drove up to the curb in front of the apartment building. The car's backseat passenger door opened and a young boy jumped out. "See ya!" he yelled. The driver, a woman, waved at Logan.

The young boy with tousled blond hair ran to Logan and threw his arms around Logan's neck. "Daddy, we went to see a soccer game. It was great. I ate some popcorn."

"That sounds like fun. Looks like you've been rolling in the dirt," Logan said.

"Yeah, sort of." The boy turned to Zoey.

"Hi," he said.

Zoey smiled. "Hi."

The boy walked over to her and stuck out his hand. "I'm Charles Howard Reid. I'm five. You can call me Charlie."

Zoey grinned and shook his hand. "I'm Zoey Lorraine Corban. I'm twenty-nine. You can call me Zoey."

"Zoey's going to live here," Logan said. "She's moving into 1-C."

Charlie nodded seriously. "Good. Tick and Bugger weren't very nice."

Zoey snorted. "Tick and Bugger?" She looked over at Logan. He rolled his eyes.

"Yes," Charlies said seriously. "I didn't like them. They were mean, and they yelled at me. I think I'll like you better."

"I already like you," Zoey smiled. "Was that your mother dropping you off?" She glanced at Logan. "Joint custody?" she asked.

"No, that's Javie's mom," Charlie said. "My mom is dead."

Zoey gasped. Logan could see a look of real distress on her face.

"I'm so sorry," she said.

"My mom had the analism."

Logan stared down at the papers on the table. "Aneurysm," he said quietly.

"In her head," Charlie continued.

"Brain aneurysm," Logan's voice was low. He glanced at Zoey. Her hand was over her heart, her eyes darting between him and Charlie.

"I'm so very sorry. So sorry. I know how you feel," she said to Charlie.

"You do?" Charlie said. "Did your mom die, too?"

Zoey shook her head. "No, not my mom. My son. My son died."

Logan jerked his head toward her, a piercing look in his eyes. Zoey was slumped forward now, smile gone, a deeply sad look on her face. He saw her reach up and brush a tear away.

"Did he have the brain analism?" Charlie's voice was gentle.

"No. He was sick, in and out of the hospital most of his life. He died in the hospital when he was just three years old. His name was Joshua, and we called him Josh."

Logan could feel a familiar pain in his heart.

All was quiet for a moment. Then Charlie stepped up to Zoey and put his arms around her neck in a gentle hug. Zoey returned the hug.

Finally the two pulled apart. "I feel better now," Zoey said.

"I do, too," Charlie responded. "I'm glad you're going to live here."

"I'm glad, too." Zoey smiled.

Logan was surprised to realize that he felt glad, too. He remained quiet.

Zoey stood. "Okay. I'm going home now." She turned to Logan. "I'll read the lease carefully, sign both copies, and return one to you this week with my deposit."

She headed toward the sidewalk, turned back and said to Charlie, "Nice to meet you, Charles Howard Reid. Let's go to a soccer game together sometime."

Charlie began jumping up and down. He turned to his dad. "Can I? Can I? Can I go with Zoey to the soccer game?"

Logan smiled. "Yes, but after Zoey moves in."

Charlie turned back to Zoey and called out, "Hurry up! Hurry and move in! Hurry up!"

Zoey laughed and nodded as she waved goodbye.

Charlie returned to Logan, leaned up against his dad, and put his arm around Logan's neck. "I like Zoey."

Logan pulled Charlie onto his lap. "I like her, too," he replied.

After a long moment, Logan put Charlie down and gathered his book and papers. "Come on, Charlie. It's getting dark. Let's try to come up with something good to make for dinner. You can help me. Okay?"

"Okay," Charlie said. "Can we have some ice cream?"

"Not before supper. You can have some for dessert if we have any. Let's go look in the freezer. And you need to take a bath."

4 Sunday Potluck

Gwilym parked his car in front of the apartment building. Dusk had fallen, and he could see a light in the window of the upstairs apartment, Nina's apartment. He smiled. He gathered his grocery bags, went up the front steps, through the front door, and up the flight of stairs just inside. He stopped and put his bags down at Nina's door, 2-A. He paused and took a deep breath, then knocked on the door.

Seconds later, Nina threw open the door, a big smile on her lovely face.

"Gwilym! Come on in. What do you have there?"

"Some wine for dinner and some ice cream for Logan's little boy." He found himself unaccountably pleased at her welcome. "And for us, too. I bought two big tubs."

"Excellent. I suggest you go down to Logan's right away and give him the ice cream. I don't have any room in my freezer, and I'm quite sure that Logan will make room for the ice cream. Charlie loves ice cream."

Gwilym followed her instructions. Thirty seconds later, Charlie opened the door when Gwilym knocked on 1-A.

"Hi. Who are you?" Charlie asked.

"I'm Gwilym. I've been invited to dinner. I brought ice cream."

Charlie began jumping up and down and squealing. "Yay! Ice cream!"

Gwilym laughed just as Logan appeared at the door.

"Hey, Gwilym."

"Nina told me to bring this ice cream to you. She doesn't have room in her freezer."

Charlie was zooming around the living room now, arms out, pretending to be an airplane or a bird or something. "Ice cream! Ice cream!"

"You know how to make an entrance," Logan said.

"Not really an entrance yet. I'm going back up to Nina's apartment. We'll see you in a little while."

Logan took the grocery bag with the ice cream. "Very good. Come back by six thirty. We'll eat here at my place because it's too chilly tonight to eat outside." He turned to the zooming boy. "Charlie, calm down." Logan closed the door.

Gwilymn could hear Logan say, "Time to take a bath."

"I don't want to take a bath," Charlie whined.

"If you don't, no one will want to sit next to you at dinner because you're so dirty."

"Zoey hugged me. She didn't think I was too dirty."

"That's different. Go run some water in the tub. Get cleaned up and then come back and help me set the table. And be sure to use soap to wash, not just water."

"I know! I'm not a baby!" Charlie said as he headed for the bathroom.

Logan chuckled. "And put on clean clothes after your bath. Clean clothes, not those dirty clothes!"

By that time, Gwilym was half way up the stairs where he found Nina's door open. He walked into her apartment.

"Nina. I'm here. I left the ice cream with Logan." He looked around. The apartment was lovely. There were big windows on the south and west, an open living-dining area, a compact kitchen, and at the back of the apartment, doors to what appeared to be two bedrooms and a bath.

"Come on in, Gwilym. I roasted a chicken. It's almost done."

"You have two bedrooms?"

"Yes, I used to have a roommate when we were both university students, but she graduated and got a job in Phoenix. Logan and I have the biggest apartments in the building. The other apartments only have one bedroom. Sit down and answer some questions for me."

Gwilymn chuckled, "Some questions? Okay. Ask away."

"What's your last name again? I was so upset after Vic was shot that I can't remember anything."

"My last name is Havard."

"And you're Canadian?"

"That's right. I come down to Tucson every winter for the jazz fest and to enjoy the warm weather. I'm from Vancouver."

"I've heard Vancouver is really beautiful. I've never been there. What's Vancouver like?"

"My hometown is a fairly large city, nearly seven hundred thousand, and over two million if you count the entire metro area. Because we're on the ocean, the climate is fairly mild. The population is very ethnically diverse. And yes, Vancouver has been described by many as a very beautiful city."

"Sounds lovely. What do you do there?"

Gwilym hesitated. What would she think if she knew how deep he was into the jazz scene?

"I have a couple of businesses."

"Like what?"

"A bookstore. And a night club. A jazz club."

"Oh, cool!" Nina grinned. "Like the club is dedicated to jazz?"

"That's right." He paused. "I want to say again how very much I enjoy your music. Your jazz lines are the best."

"Oh, so Mr. Havard knows the jazz language."

"I do. And I find the name of your group to be very clever."

"So you know about the classic…"

"'Take Five'. Dave Brubeck Quartet. Yes, a classic."

"Most people don't get that. They don't know enough about jazz to understand the connection." She paused. "Now we're only three, not four. I don't know how long it will take for Vic to get back to his bass."

"Let's go visit Vic tomorrow if the doctor will allow it. Or the next day. We'll ask Logan to go, too."

"Okay."

"I'm hoping he can give us some useful information. Logan and I are trying to figure out what that man with the gun wanted. Like what does 'one down' mean?"

"I really have no idea." Nina was frowning now. "Let's don't talk about this at dinner. I don't want Charlie to be upset."

"Then ask me some more questions." He smiled, hoping to distract her.

"Okay. Do you live in a house or an apartment or a school bus or a tent?" She grinned.

"An apartment. And I drive a Toyota."

"What do you do for fun?"

"Sometimes I go hiking in the mountains or kayaking off the coast. And I go to jazz festivals in interesting places. Like Tucson, Arizona."

"Do you have a wife or a girlfriend?"

"No. Do you?"

"No. I'm not married. No wife. No girlfriend." She giggled.

Gwilym smiled. "Boyfriend? Husband?"

"Nope." She added, "I had a boyfriend, but I don't have one now."

He nodded and grinned.

"I'm curious about something, but I can't think of a clever way to ask." Nina was looking at him intently now.

"Let me guess. You want to know about my ethnicity. So ask me this, 'Gwilym, what is your middle name?'"

Nina chuckled. "Okay. What is your middle name, Gwilym Havard?"

"Sanjay."

"Sanjay? That's an Indian name."

"Right. My mom is originally from the state of Tamil Nadu in India. She came to Vancouver to study at the University of British Columbia. She met my dad, they married, and after a few years, I came into the world."

"That's so sweet. I wondered because you're too dark to really be Welsh or English or something. And you don't look Mexican or African American. Or African Canadian. I was just curious. Looks like everything turned out well."

"What do you mean?"

"Indian mom and Canadian dad together made a handsome son." Nina put her hand over her mouth for a moment. "Don't listen to me. I talk too much."

Gwilym chuckled. "Thanks for the compliment. For the record, I think you are beautiful. Very beautiful."

"Oh jeez. I'm pretty ordinary when we go to Italy."

"Your family is Italian?"

"On my mother's side. There are lots of beautiful women, and men, too, in Italy. Are there a lot of ethnic Indians in Vancouver?"

"Quite a few, but the biggest ethnic group is Chinese. Many are from Hong Kong."

"Interesting. I hope I get to go to Vancouver someday."

"I have a question for you."

"Go ahead."

"Now you know my middle name. What is your middle name, Nina Perry? And did you grow up here?"

"Oh, you know what my middle name is." She rolled her eyes.

"I do? No, I don't. Give me a clue."

Nina looked at him, her eyes half closed, and she sang in a sultry voice, "And I'm feeling good."

Gwilym burst into laughter. "Of course, of course. I'm an idiot. Nina Simone Perry. What a great name. I take it your parents were jazz fans."

Nina was grinning now. "Yes, both my parents were crazy about Nina Simone. Actually my dad is a jazz musician. He played piano like me. I was born and spent much of my childhood and early teen years in New York City. We moved out here to Tucson when I was in high school."

A bell on the stove rang.

"Oh," Nina jumped up. "The chicken is done." She pulled the oven door open and pulled out a baking pan with a nicely roasted chicken in it.

"Oh, that smells great," Gwilym said. "I'm starving."

"Then let's get everything together and go down to Logan's apartment."

~~~

Nina brought the chicken in the pan it was baked in, holding it with thick oven mitts. Gwilym brought the wine. When they arrived at Logan's, the door was ajar. Gwilym could hear people talking. He knocked, and they walked into Logan's apartment.

Several faces turned to Nina and called out, "Hey, Nina!"

"Hey to you, too." Nina grinned. "Here's the roasted chicken. Okay to put it on the table, Logan?"

"Sure. I left a space right in the middle of the table with a trivet. I'll get a knife to cut it."

Nina turned to the others. "I want to introduce Gwilym to you. This is Gwilym Havard. He's from Vancouver, B. C., he's a big jazz fan, and he brought wine!"

"And ice cream!" Charlie called out in a loud voice. Everyone laughed.

"Let me introduce everyone." Nina pointed to a young man. "This is Li. His actual name is Liang but Li is easier. He's Chinese American."

To Gwilym, it was obvious Li was Asian with his epicanthal eye fold. His dark hair was pulled back in a tight knot, and he had a goatee and mustache on his handsome face. There was something very familiar about him. Gwilym couldn't think what exactly. He'd never before met Li.

Gwilym and Li shook hands.

"Li is a very, very excellent chef at one of Tucson's top Chinese restaurants," Nina added.

The young man nodded. "Yes, I'm a chef. I have a new gig, too, part-time. I'm a model."

"A model of what?" Nina asked.

"Clothing. Designer clothes. Hip men's clothing, if you prefer. Like I model purple suits."

Everyone laughed.

"Don't laugh," Li grinned. "It's easy. I put on these clothes, I have the pleasure of holding some scantily-clad females in my arms, they take my photo, and I get paid for just standing there. Paid well, I might add."

"Cool!" one of the others said. Gwilym noted that the speaker was a woman slightly older than the others, at least mid-thirties. She had on some rather dramatic clothing, colorful and draped. Her hair was a mass of dark curls.

"This is Frida."

Gwilym shook her hand.

"Frida is a bartender. But her real job is to make trouble." Nina grinned.

Frida nodded and smiled. "Yep. I'm an activist. I like to organize protests."

"What do you protest?" Gwilym asked.

"Whatever needs protesting. Human rights or social justice issues, lack of action on climate change, the price of lettuce too high, or wages too low." Everyone nodded.

"And this is Dylan."

Gwilym turned to a mid-height woman with long auburn hair about the same age as the others. She was dressed in jeans and a long-sleeve cotton t-shirt. She stuck out her hand and smiled. Gwilym shook her hand, too.

"Dylan is an accountant so she's good with numbers. Dylan used to be a tattoo artist, but then she went back to school so she could learn how to count money. But before she did that, she gave me a great tattoo. I'll show you my tattoo later. I'm very proud of it." Nina grinned.

Gwilym felt himself getting warm. Where exactly on her body was this tattoo? Maybe he would get a chance to find out, maybe even to see it.

Logan removed the apron from his waist. "That's all of us for now. We have another resident here, Marc, who is a photojournalist. He's supposed to come home soon. And Nina's friend Zoey is going to move into the empty apartment downstairs. We'll be seven adults and one child when we're all here." He looked around. "Are we ready to eat?"

"Yes!" everyone said at once.

Gwilym was seated across from Nina, which he liked. He could see her better than if he were sitting on the same side of the table. Logan was at the head of the table, and Charlies was at the other end. The table was full of dishes.

The table was full of dishes. Two big salads, tabouli, a rice and bean dish that Logan had made, a bowl of steamed vegetables, Nina's chicken, an apple pie, and something Li had made which he called "baozi." It sounded like "bow-zuh" to Gwilym's ears. Baozi looked to Gwilym like a small bun with different kinds of fillings. Very good. Everything was very good.

Gwilym brought out his wine and opened a bottle. Everyone held out a wine glass. When the wine glasses were full, Logan looked at Nina and said, "Want to make a toast to Vic?"

Nina stood and held up her wine glass. "To my friend and bassist Vic. I hope the best for him always." Everyone around the table held their glasses up and nodded their approval.

Time to eat. They all ate with relish. The conversation was light and pleasant, mostly about the warm winter weather, the recent jazz fest, an upcoming mariachi concert, and a bicycling event.

Finally, when they were finished eating, Charlie looked at Gwilym. "Do we ever get to eat that ice cream ever?" Gwilym looked at Logan, but he was already on his feet fetching the ice cream.

"You go first, Charlie," Gwilym said. "Do you prefer chocolate or pistachio?"

Charlie had a stricken look on his face. "I don't know what that is pis...pis...ice cream."

"Piss ice cream," Li repeated. "Try that one, Charlie." The adults chuckled.

Logan said, "Here, I'll give you a spoonful and you can see if you like it."

Charlie tasted the ice cream. "Oh, that's good! Can I have that?"

"Please," Logan said.

"Please," Charlie repeated. Logan gave him a small bowl full of pistachio ice cream.

Another round of wine and ice cream, and finally Logan said. "Charlie, it's after eight. You have to get up early and go to school in the morning. Say goodnight to everyone. Put on your pajamas and I'll come and tuck you in."

Charlie made his way around the table and hugged everyone goodnight, including Gwilym. He headed to his bedroom.

"Back in a minute," Logan said.

The others got up and began carrying dishes to the kitchen. They took turns washing and drying the dishes and putting leftovers away.

Logan returned after a while. "Thanks, everyone. Let's go sit in the living room. Bring the wine."

They all sat in a big circle in Logan's living room. There was a sofa and several soft chairs. A large arched window looked out over the street in front of their building.

Logan began. "Now that Mr. Motor Mouth has gone to bed, I'd like to bring up what happened to Vic." He looked at Li, Dylan, and Frida. "You know about this, right?"

All three nodded. "Awful," Frida said.

"Does Vic have any enemies?" Li asked.

Nina shook her head. "Everyone loves Vic. He never said anything about having a problem with anyone."

"But maybe that's not something he would talk about," Logan said. "I think we should go see him in the hospital and ask him a few questions. But only when he's well enough to see visitors."

Gwilym nodded. "I guess most of us have had things happen in our lives that were not pleasant. He might have some insight into who could have something against him. He may have been a victim of race-based harassment. I've had some experience with that myself."

Nina frowned. "Gwilym's mom is from India. He's kind of darker than some of us."

"We could talk to Vic's wife, too," Gwilym added.

"And we need to stay in touch with the cops and see if they are learning anything new," Logan said.

"I've been thinking about this," Dylan said. "The gunman called out 'one down' before he shot Vic. Any ideas about what this might mean?"

Everyone shook their heads 'no.'

Logan said, "That he said those words makes me very uncomfortable. It sounds like the shooter has some kind of agenda, and his agenda might include other people. I mean, is there a number two? For sure, we don't want him gunning down anyone else. Has anyone heard any news about another shooting or even another person being attacked, beaten up or whatever."

More negative responses.

"Okay, I guess we'll have to wait until we talk to Vic. And talk to the cops, too," Logan said. "Anyone have other news to share?"

"Well, I already told you about my modeling gig," Li said.

"I'm ramping up for tax season," Dylan smiled. "When all the tax forms go in, I may take a little vacation."

"Oh, gosh," Nina responded. "I don't know how you do that, Dylan. All those numbers would make my eyes cross."

"The great thing about numbers is the simplicity. Either you get it right or you get it wrong. Not at all like what Logan does."

Gwilym looked at Logan. "What do you do?"

"I'm finishing my doctoral degree in philosophy. My area of interest is ethics. Applied ethics, specifically. That means applying ethical concepts to the idea of human rights, for one example."

"Yeah, ethics like whether or not people should get a livable wage," Frida said, her voice edgy. "Of course they should get a livable wage! I've had some good talks with Logan about human rights."

"And animal rights, too," added Dylan. "That's an interest of mine. I'm actually thinking of doing some volunteer work in this area."

"So you are all really a group of intellectuals?" Gwilym asked.

"Not me," Li said, "I'm a foodie. I think Charlie and I are on the same page. Does it taste good? That's what Charlie and I want to know."

Nina sighed. "I'm no intellectual. I just like getting carried away on the tunes."

"Your jazz lines." Gwilym smiled.

"Yes, my jazz lines. Speaking of which, Gwilym, it's about time for us to go to the club."

Logan turned to the others and said, "This thing with Vic happened. And on top of that, Gwilym saw some dude follow Nina home last night so he's going to escort her to and from the club tonight."

"Thanks, Gwilym. That's good of you," Frida said. Dylan nodded her agreement.

Nina and Gwilym left first, walking away from the apartments toward Fourth Avenue.

The others all said goodnight to each other, leaving Logan alone with his sleeping child.

5 Visiting Vic

Logan groaned, rolled onto his side, and opened his eyes. Six thirty in the morning. He sighed. Time to get up. He had a little over an hour to get himself and Charlie up and going, then twenty minutes to walk to Charlie's school. Logan suddenly remembered the cleaners and the workmen who were coming this morning to do repairs on the apartment that was going to be Zoey's. He sighed again, threw off the covers, and pulled himself up and out of bed.

After a very quick shower, he started a pot of coffee, left his apartment and went down the hall to unlock the back door so the workers could enter through the laundry room. Next he unlocked the door to apartment 1-C. He went back to his apartment and looked at the clock on the bookshelf. Time to wake Charlie. He went into his room and gently touched Charlie's shoulder. "Time to get up."

Charlie sighed and rolled toward his dad. "I'm sleepy."

"You'll wake up fast. Get up and get dressed. I'll fix you some breakfast."

Charlie sat up. "Can I have some of that good cereal, the one with the little rings that come in different colors? It's really good."

"That cereal is not good for you. Too much sugar. I don't have any of that crap anyway."

"That's what Zoey eats."

"What? How do you know what Zoey eats?" Logan was trying not to laugh.

"She *might* eat that cereal."

"I seriously doubt that. Don't make up stuff unless you're writing a novel. You can ask her what she really eats after she moves in. Get up, get dressed, and come to the table."

"What's a novel?"

"A made-up story in a book, not something you tell your dad. You tell me the truth. Always. And the truth is that you don't know what Zoey eats for breakfast. Here's your choices. I have a veggie frittata with cheese in it. I made it last night. Or you can have some avocado with cream cheese on whole wheat toast, or some oatmeal with nuts and fruit."

"Veggie frittata." Charlie was on his feet now. Not long after, he was seated at the table eating his breakfast.

"I'll be back in a minute, Charlie," Logan said. "The workmen are here to fix up Zoey's apartment, and I want to see if they need anything."

Charlie nodded, ate another bite of frittata and drank some milk.

What is all this about Zoey? Logan wondered, as he walked down the hall to apartment 1-C. The cleaners were already there and had moved almost all of the trash and broken furniture outside. There were two of them, and now they were piling everything into a trailer behind a pickup truck. Almost immediately he encountered the foreman of the repair team, José Something. Logan couldn't remember his name. The property owners, not Logan, had hired both the cleaners and also José and his team. They were already carrying tools and materials in through the laundry room back door.

"How are things going?" Logan asked. "Do you need anything from me?"

"No. We're just bringing in what we need. We're used to working without any input so we'll be okay."

That sounded to Logan like 'go away and leave us alone so we can do our job.' "Okay, see you later."

Logan returned to his apartment and went into the next phase of getting ready for school. He made sure Charlie brushed his teeth and had everything he needed for school in his backpack. Logan locked the door to their apartment, and they set off walking to the north.

"What are you going to do today?" Logan asked.

"We're learning numbers. So I guess we'll do that some more. Did you know if you put one in front of zero it turns it into ten?"

"Hmmm...and two in front of zero makes twenty?"

Charlie frowned. "I guess so. We didn't talk about two. And I think my teacher is going to read us a novel."

"Oh, really?" Logan chuckled.

"She always reads us a book at story time."

Logan nodded. "Good. Stories are fun to hear."

Two kindergarten teachers were waiting outside the school door, welcoming students.

"Hi Charlie! Hi Mr. Reid!" The teacher was a young and very enthusiastic Mexican-American named Miss Acevedo. "Charlie, guess what? We're going to have story hour today, and later in the afternoon, a mariachi band is going to play for the whole school."

"Great!" Charlie was already skipping into the building and waving at a friend. "Bye, Daddy," he called as he skipped away.

"Is everything going okay?" Logan asked the teacher.

"Just fine. Charlie is an excellent student. He's very well-behaved most of the time. He stopped saying that word."

Logan's eyebrows went up. "What word?"

Ms. Acevedo giggled. "It starts with 'f' and ends with 'k.'"

"Oh, no." Logan shook his head in dismay. Where the hell had Charlie heard that? Logan made an effort to never curse around his son.

"Don't worry. I convinced him that he shouldn't say it because it's so rude. He's a good boy."

"Okay. Let me know if you have any problems." Logan said goodbye and waved.

He walked toward home, taking his time and thinking. A morning like this, repetitious and predictable, boring even, was his favorite kind of morning. Charlie seemed happy. Nothing bad happened. Yes, a bright, blue-sky morning full of giggling kids and quiet streets and no ambulance. No ambulance arriving to take away Charlie's mother, Logan's wife. No one dying. Caroline never coming home again.

Except...

Logan's thoughts turned to the traumatic event of yesterday. Blood streaming from Vic's chest and his heart stopping. Gwilym helping him to save Vic's life. Nina barely able to talk because she was sobbing uncontrollably. The whole thing was awful and weird. Who comes into a store and just starts shooting? Never bothers to demand money or anything else? And what on earth could that phrase "one down" mean? Then Gwilym telling him about a stranger following Nina home. Logan had an ominous feeling about that.

He returned to his apartment and poured another cup of coffee. Sometimes he could hear Nina moving around in the apartment above his place, and he almost always heard her music. She had a small digital piano that she played at home. This morning it was quiet, and he assumed she was still asleep. He wondered what had happened with Gwilym. Did he go back to his hotel or did he stay with Nina? He smiled at the thought of that. Gwilym seemed like an upright kind of guy. Nina could benefit from a good guy.

Suddenly Logan heard a saw buzzing down the hall then hammers began banging into nails. Sounds like that indicated that the repair work was progressing. The noise would wake everyone up, of course, and eventually it would annoy Logan. He decided to escape the noise, go to the community garden and check on his veggies.

The community garden was much closer to his apartment than the school. Within ten minutes, Logan had passed through the gate and was inspecting his beds. It wasn't exactly quiet in the garden. He could hear the traffic on the parkway off to the south, and he knew a train would be coming by soon. The trains were always loud although he'd heard them so many times that he'd become accustomed to them. He took a deep breath. Yes, a sunny day in January. The kale and spinach looked good. Broccoli was coming on. He'd already harvested a lot of the carrots and beets. The green peas were doing well on the trellis he'd set up in the fall. He snatched one green pea pod and crunched it in his mouth. Oh so sweet. Delicious. Why didn't more people have vegetable gardens? he wondered. The food was so good and it was so nice to be outdoors and doing something relevant. Yes, "relevant" was a good word.

Logan had come to believe that so much of what he'd done in his life had been irrelevant. He'd spent so much of his life with his nose in a book, chasing the dream of becoming a successful academic, a professor. And for what? Logan had lost one of the two most important people in his life, his beloved Caroline. Now he had the other most important person in his life, Charlie, to care for and to love. He was determined to keep Charlie safe and happy.

No more chasing "success." Focus on happiness, peace, and serenity. Those were his goals now. He was going to take Charlie on more hikes, experience the natural world more, go to more sporting events, maybe help Charlie learn a sport and be on a team. That thought brought the memory of Zoey Corban to his awareness. Soccer. Smiles. Sweet hugs for Charlie. Maybe he'd gather his courage and try to get to know Zoey a little better. For Charlie's sake, he told himself. Yeah, for Charlie.

Just at that moment, another gardener entered the community garden. Logan stood and waved. "Hi, Lucy. Haven't seen you for a while."

Lucy Sanchez was an older woman who lived in the neighborhood in a small house with a small yard. Her home was across the street and a couple of doors down from Logan's apartment building. She and Logan had traded seeds and bedding plants several times.

"Good to see you, Logan. How's your garden doing?"

"Can't complain. I'm putting kale and spinach into everything I cook because I have so much of it. I made a frittata with kale in it for breakfast."

"Same here. I'm giving away a lot of veggies to the community food bank, too. These plants produce too much for me to eat myself. I just like growing them."

"Lucy, did you hear about Vic Davis getting shot?"

"Yes, that's really terrible."

"This may seem like a strange question, but you always seemed really observant to me. Have you noticed anything weird going on in the neighborhood? Any weird people? I mean weirder than the usual crowd?"

Lucy laughed. "You mean the university students?"

Logan smiled. "Yeah, typical student weirdness. Loud parties, too much beer or whatever they are drinking these days." He looked down at his vegetable bed and then back at Lucy. She was small in stature, barely five feet tall, and her wrinkled face often had a smile on it. "I'm not sure what I mean. Something different? Strangers, maybe?"

Lucy nodded. "You know I'm indoors a lot reading or watching movies on the television. Or here in the community garden. But now that you mention it, I did see something unusual. I was out around dusk a couple of days ago. There was this man. It was the second time I'd seen him. I don't know if he lives in the neighborhood. I've never seen him entering or leaving a house or apartment. Both times he was dressed the same way, in dark clothes with that thing around his head. What do they call it? A hoodie. He sort of disappeared behind a car or an oleander bush if anyone looked his way. He appeared to be watching your apartment building."

"Can you describe him? Anything more?"

"Not quite as tall as you. Maybe five nine or ten? Slender. Dark clothes, as I said. I couldn't really see his face. I'm not sure about his age, but from the way he moved, I'd say fairly young. Twenties probably."

Logan nodded. "I'm trying to figure out what's going on and why Vic got shot. Thanks for the observations."

"Guess I better get back to weeding."

"Yeah, me, too. Nice to see you."

"You, too." Lucy moved off to her garden beds.

Logan stayed another hour in the gardens. When he returned to Casa Pacifica, the workers were still at it. He called the police station and asked to speak to anyone about how the investigation was going into the assault on Vic Davis. He was connected to a detective, but the answer was vague. Logan knew from reading the local news that the cops were busy all the time. They had a lot to deal with, and Logan didn't know if they would ever be able to identify, much less apprehend, the man who had shot Vic.

He ate some lunch and returned to his notebook of ideas on how to make a living when his teaching assistant's position was completed at the end of the semester. This time the job of ESL teacher stuck out. Yes, maybe that would be fun and pay well enough to keep his little family fed. And he'd go ahead and interview for a teaching job at the community college. Worth a try. He dozed off in his chair, and when he woke, it was time to go get Charlie.

Charlie talked all the way home about the "novel" that his teacher read to the class and about the mariachi concert. Logan fed him a snack when they arrived home. A few minutes later, Nina appeared at his door.

"Logan, I called the hospital. They said it would be okay to visit Vic this afternoon. Gwilym is coming to pick me up in a few minutes. Want to go?"

"Yes, but I don't want to take Charlie. I'll ask Frida if he can stay with her." He called Frida, she said, "Yes, of course, as long as you are back by six. I have to go to work." Charlie went to Frida's, excited because it meant he could play with Frida's new kitten. Gwilym showed up in his rental car, and Logan, Nina and Gwilym headed for the hospital. On the way there, Logan told Nina and Gwilym about his conversation with Lucy and about the man she'd seen who had been watching their apartments.

Gwilym shook his head. "I don't like the sound of that."

"Me neither," Logan said. Nina stayed quiet.

When they arrived at the hospital, they were told by the nurse in charge that they could only spend fifteen minutes with Vic. "Don't upset him with anything too serious," the nurse warned. "He's getting better, but a short, friendly and calm visit would be best for his health."

When they entered Vic's room. Vic was awake and smiling.

Nina went to his side and took his hand in hers. Logan and Gwilym stood at the foot of his bed.

"Hello," Vic said. His voice was weak. "Thanks for coming to visit me. And even more important, thanks for saving my life. They told me how you guys stopped the bleeding and got me breathing again. I can't thank you enough." Logan and Gwilym nodded. Vic turned to Nina. "I'm sorry, Nina. You'll have to do without a bass for a while."

Nina brushed away tears. "Focus on getting better, Vic. We'll be so glad when you are ready to play again. Until then, we'll miss you. The music won't be the same without you."

"Thanks, Nina. My wife is getting the kids from school now and feeding them supper. She'll be back this evening. She's bringing me some music to listen to. Ron Carter."

"You can't go wrong with Ron Carter. If you need anything, tell Joanie to call me," Nina said.

"Vic, do you think you'd be up for helping us figure out what the hell happened? Who that shooter was and what he wanted?" Logan asked.

"I've been going over that again and again," Vic said, his voice serious. "He just walked in, pulled out the gun and started shooting. He made no attempt to steal anything. I don't get it. I mean, he could have forced me to open the cash register, but he didn't. He didn't even look at the cash register."

"Any idea what he meant by 'one down'? We've been been trying to figure that out." Logan gestured to Gwilym.

Vic shook his head. "No. I've wondered about that myself. One of the Tucson police detectives came by again and ask me about that, too. He said they don't have any leads. The shooter just disappeared into thin air."

"Have you had any conflicts with anyone lately?" Logan asked. "Any group or groups you are a member of that have had some kind of problem? Because 'one down' sounds way too much like there may be more targets." He paused. "I don't really know what to ask you."

"No." Vic shook his head. "I'm pretty busy working at the convenience store and playing with Nina and the cats in our group. I guess maybe there's been a customer who wasn't happy with the convenience store service or a product or something. But I'm pretty sure my boss would have told me about that and warned me if a customer was being aggressive. I go to church on Sunday with my wife and kids. That's about it for social life. I thought I got along well with everyone. I'm really sorry. I wish I could be of more help."

Gwilym spoke up. "You're a black man, an African American. I'm obviously not a white man, or at least that's what most people think. I'm too dark to pass for white. Do you think this attack may have been racially motivated? That's happened to me. I got beat up once pretty bad by some white supremacists."

Nina looked at him, a sad expression on her face.

Vic shrugged his shoulders. "Not in recent years. I was born and grew up in a small town in New Jersey. There was this group of white boys who used to harass black kids in the school, including me. Once I got beat up pretty bad, too. Why are you dark? You don't look black. I thought maybe you're Mexican."

"I'm Canadian. My dad is white northern European and my mom is from India, from a part of India where the people are pretty dark-skinned."

Vic nodded. "Okay. I see. Learn something every day. I guess I've never known anyone with family from India. I've never had any race problem like that since moving out here to Tucson. How about you?"

"No. Everyone here has been very kind to me." Gwilym glanced over at Nina and smiled. "My incident happened in Sweden, of all places. I went there for a jazz festival and ran into a bunch of white supremacists having a demonstration on the street."

Just at that moment, the nurse came into the room and said, "Okay, folks. Time to say goodbye. Mr. Davis gets his meds now, and then we'll bring him something to eat."

"Thank you all again," Vic said. "You've been great. I would not have survived without you. And thanks for coming by this evening. If I think of anything helpful, I'll text Nina and she can share with you."

They left the hospital and drove back to the apartment building in silence. When they arrived, Logan said, "I'm going to continue thinking about this and investigating in whatever way I can. I just have this gut feeling something is going on."

Gwilym nodded. He didn't mention that seeing Nina being followed was on his mind, too.

And Logan remembered what Lucy Sanchez had told him about the stranger in their neighborhood who was watching the apartments.

"What are you going to do this evening?" Nina asked Logan.

"Feed Charlie. Watch cartoons or a kids' movie with him. Read him a story and hope he goes to sleep early."

"Sounds exciting," Nina chuckled.

"Lately we've been watching basketball games, which is a lot more exciting than cartoons. For me anyway. I played basketball in high school, and I never get tired of the game. When Charlie gets a little older, we'll go to some Arizona Wildcat games on the university campus. I bet he'll like that. How about you, Nina? What are you going to do?"

"I'm taking her out to dinner and then to the club." Gwilym smiled.

Nina laughed. "Can't say no to that."

"I approve." Logan smiled. "Have fun."

6 TWO DOWN

As Nina and Gwilym left the Casa Pacifica apartments, Li called out to them. "Hey, wait a minute, and I'll walk with you." He joined them, and all three headed for Fourth Avenue.

"What are you doing this evening?" Nina asked.

"Meeting a girl." Li laughed. "I like girls." He stroked his goatee and winked.

Nina grinned and said to Gwilym, "Li is popular with the ladies. He's so handsome, even without his purple designer suit."

Li grinned. "Guess I'm pretty boring tonight." He was dressed in blue jeans, a red t-shirt, and a black leather jacket. His dark hair was pulled back into a knot at the back of his head as usual.

"I think you're handsome anyway, even in blue jeans," Nina said.

"What are you two doing? Isn't it a little early to start your gig at the jazz club?" Li asked.

"Gwilym is taking me out to dinner first. He's interested in our Sonoran cuisine," she said.

"Yeah, right. I bet that's not all he's interested in." Li looked over at Gwilym, then winked at Nina. He turned his attention back to Gwilym. "Before you go back to Canada, come by the restaurant where I'm the chef. You won't be disappointed."

"Definitely," Gwilym nodded. "I'm a big fan of Chinese foods."

"I'm going to move ahead of you. I want to be there when my girl arrives. See ya." Li waved goodbye and started off at a brisk pace.

Gwilym looked around. It was a chilly January evening, already well past sunset. He was always surprised at how warm the days were in sunny southern Arizona and how cold the nights could be.

"I like going on a slow walk because this neighborhood is interesting to me. It's a combination of small, older homes mixed in with apartments and businesses. I've seen a tattoo business, a dance studio, an architect's office, and there's a grocery store over there." Gwilym pointed across the street.

"Yes, it's a coffee shop, too."

"This part of the city is lively with people on the streets, and yet it seems somehow set apart from the larger metro area."

"I guess that's because Tucson has a lot of areas that used to be separated but have come together through urban growth. My parents live in a part of town on the east side that used to be small ranches. There's more space in their neighborhood. I mean there are really big lots, sometimes a quarter or a half an acre. The Apaches used to raid over there. They liked to steal horses."

"Interesting. I guess this means I need to read up on the history of Tucson."

"Oh, so you sometimes think about things other than jazz?"

He could tell Nina was teasing him. "Occasionally. But I'll admit, jazz always comes first."

By this time, they had arrived at Fourth Avenue. They wandered north, holding hands as they looked in shop windows, until they came to the restaurant Gwilym had chosen.

After they were seated, Gwilym said, "How about if you decide what we should eat? I've never been to Mexico, and I don't know much about the food. What do you recommend?"

Nina looked over the menu.

"We'll start with *pozole*, then move on to a couple of different kinds of *tacos* and *burritos*, then *quesedilla*, and *chimichanga*, too, and *arroz con frijoles y salsa*. Oh, and an *enchilada*. We'll come back another time and try the *mole*. For now, we'll just get one or two of each and share. Okay?"

Gwilym grinned. "I have no idea what you just said except the word 'share' so you'll have to tell me what I'm eating as we go."

"Fine. And we'll finish with some *helado*. That's ice cream."

"And I'll be so full, I won't be able to walk out of here."

Nina laughed. "Yes, you will. Don't forget. We have to get to the club by nine. Jazz is on the menu there."

"Best dish ever." He reached out and took her hand in his. "Thank you, Nina Simone Perry."

While they were waiting for the food, Gwilym entertained Nina with stories about his trips to international jazz festivals. "I've been to several in Europe. Berlin, Copenhagen, Montreux in Switzerland, Stockholm in Sweden."

"That's where you were attacked?"

"Yes, they beat me up pretty bad. I had to spend a couple of days in the hospital."

"I'm so sorry that happened," Nina said. "You're not even really dark dark. Not like Miles Davis. He was really dark. And handsome, too. Oh, he could play that horn. I love listening to Miles."

Gwilym shrugged. "I was darker than those racists who attacked me. That's all they cared about."

Nina had a thoughtful look on her face. "It's your eyes. That's what's different about you." She fell silent for a moment. "I'm going to write a tune for you and call it 'India Eyes.'" She grinned.

"Wow!" Gwilym didn't know what to say. What an honor.

"I'll start working on that. Tell me about what other jazz festivals you've attended."

Gwilym nodded. "I've been to Japan for two jazz festivals, once in Tokyo and once at Mount Fuji. But I've never made it to Australia. Cancun, Mexico is on my list, too."

"What about jazz festivals in the U.S.?"

"Monterrey, a couple of times. Also New Orleans, Memphis, Newport in Rhode Island twice, and my favorite, Tucson. And, of course, Montreal and Vancouver in Canada."

Nina nodded. "You must be rich to be able to travel that much."

"Not rich. I just prioritize. I don't have a fancy car or a condo or whatever. I live a simple life. My club and the bookstore provide a regular income plus I wrote a book about jazz history and that makes a little money, too."

"You wrote a book! I'm impressed."

"I'm working on a second book now. It's about Charles Mingus. You know he was born in Nogales?"

"Yes, my dad told me that. Mingus was a great jazz musician."

"Enough about me. Tell me about you."

Nina shrugged. "Not much to tell. I learned how to play piano in elementary school, got started in jazz in middle school, and that's what I've been doing ever since. We moved to Tucson when I was in high school after my brother died."

"Oh, sorry to hear that."

"He died in a car wreck. It hit my parents and me pretty hard. So we moved here and started a new life. I finished high school here and now I take classes part time at the university. Also I work at a bookstore and teach piano to a couple of students. I don't have much money so I don't travel."

"Have you ever considered playing in a jazz festival somewhere other than Tucson?"

"I'd love to do that, but it would mean the organizers would have to pay all my travel expenses. For me and my band members, too."

Gwilym nodded. He was quite capable of doing just that. He wanted to know more about Nina. A lot more.

"Tell me about the people in your apartment building. It seems you are more than just friends."

Nina nodded. "Yes, we've formed sort of a family. Logan is the big brother who tries to take care of all of us."

"So he's more than just the manager?"

"Yes. Logan and his wife, Caroline, moved in downstairs when he was hired as the manager. I moved in later, and I had a roommate who was a student, like me. Charlie arrived later. One-by-one we ended up with the group we have now except for two very annoying students downstairs who caused a lot of trouble. They just moved out recently, and now Zoey is moving in."

"What happened to Logan's wife?"

"She died suddenly. Charlie was only two when a blood vessel ruptured in Caroline's brain. She passed out and never woke up. Logan hasn't been the same since. He used to be light-hearted and joke around a lot. Now he's often very serious. He takes good care of Charlie, and he tries to take care of everybody else, too. I think this problem with Vic is weighing on him."

"It's weighing on me, too." Gwilym frowned. "I don't want anything bad to happen to you."

Nina grinned. "Personally, I think it's really good that Zoey is moving in. She likes Logan. She told me so. And I saw the way Logan looked at her."

"Oh, yeah? Like how?"

"Well, you know Logan is a really good-looking guy with that sun-streaked hair, his green eyes, and those adorable granny glasses he wears when he's reading. So cute. Lots of women find him attractive, and it's obvious to me that Zoey is one of them. But all this time, he's never shown any interest in anyone until Zoey came along. He looks at her sideways and turns pink." Nina giggled.

"So sideways glances and pink means he likes her?" Gwilym found this very entertaining, learning what women notice when an attraction occurs between a man and a woman.

"Yes, I think he does like her. But will he follow up? He told me once he didn't want a series of women coming and going because that would be confusing for Charlie. But, down deep, I think he doesn't want to have his heart broken again. Caroline's death was really hard on him." She paused. "Hmm… I think I'm going to encourage Logan and Zoey to get to know each other better."

"Do I turn pink when I look at you?" He couldn't help but tease her a little.

Nina laughed. "Just the opposite. *I'm* the one who turns pink when I look at *you!*" She grinned. "I'd say you turn a dark red."

"Oh, gosh." Gwilym laughed. "Dark red is very revealing. I guess that means I must like you."

"I must like you, too." Nina smiled. "So tell me about you."

"I was born and grew up in Vancouver. My degree in music history is from the University of British Columbia with a minor in business admin. I told you about my club and bookstore. You already know about my parents. I have a little sister, Julie. She's into science and wants to be a marine biologist. She's still in high school." Gwilym wondered how much he should tell Nina. Might as well go for it. "I used to be married. I was married for five years. We found out pretty quickly that we were not very compatible, and finally, we just decided to call it quits. We have a friendly but distant relationship."

"I've never been married. I had a serious boyfriend, but he started hitting me. He had these temper tantrums, rages really, and he would haul off and hit me in the face."

Gwilym's eyebrows went up, and he shook his head. "Outrageous."

"Yeah, I finally escaped him. Logan helped me get away from him. That was a couple of years ago."

"How did Logan help?"

"He came over with his car. You know I don't have a car. He helped me pack and carry stuff to the car to haul over to Casa Pacifica, and he arranged for me to have a roommate, too, to reduce my expenses. My boyfriend, I mean my ex-boyfriend, came back when we were packing up. He saw what I was doing, and he got really pissed off. He started yelling at me, and he said that everything was my fault. Then he grabbed me and started shaking me. Logan saw that and pushed him away, and when my ex resisted, Logan twisted his arm and threw him to the floor."

"Whoa. Logan has always seemed so mild-mannered."

"He is most of the time. But he doesn't like seeing his friends get pushed around. Logan told my ex that I was getting a restraining order against him. My ex got up and left. I didn't hear from him again. I heard later that he moved to California."

"And you're not seeing anyone now?"

"Actually I am." Nina wiggled her eyebrows. "He's this really handsome Canadian who loves jazz. He's very nice. I like him a lot."

Gwilym, not a person prone to blushing, found himself getting very warm. "You're making me happy."

"I'm happy, too."

"And this is why you think of Logan as your big brother?"

"Yes, I love Logan. He's the best."

Two waiters showed up at that moment, each carrying a large tray with several dishes. They both dug into the food.

Half an hour later, Gwilym sat back and sighed. "Delicious food, Nina. I really liked everything. Thanks for introducing me to such excellent Mexican food."

"Sure. Tucson has some wonderful restaurants so we can try more places, including Li's Chinese restaurant, too."

More than an hour after they arrived, Gwilym and Nina left the restaurant, completely stuffed. The walk to the jazz club didn't take long. They found the club nearly empty, with lights low except for the bar and the stage lights. Nina waved to the manager behind the bar.

"I arranged to meet with Santiago and Zeke backstage," Nina said. "I'm going to see if they've arrived yet. We have to come up with some strategies for how to deal with no bass."

Gwilym was already seated at a table near the back of the club. Nina leaned down and kissed him on his cheek. He had a sudden urge to pull her close to him for a deep kiss, but he decide he'd best not. She needed to fall into the music so she could forget about her worries. He would just be a distraction.

Nina went up the short steps to the stage just as her band mates appeared. They disappeared behind the curtains. The club began to fill slowly, and the bar opened. Gwilym ordered a beer, and sat back, waiting for the music to begin.

The first set was a little rowdy because the crowd was a little rowdy. Too much booze, Gwilym decided. One obviously drunk man stood and called out to Nina between tunes, "Nina, I love you!" Then he sat down hard. His friends had to keep him on his chair and off the floor. When Nina blew the man a kiss, he attempted to stand up, but he fell down again, this time all the way to the floor. The crowd laughed.

Take Four took a short break, and Nina and her band members went back stage. Gwilym had known that this was going to happen. If Nina came and sat with him, she would be approached by customers constantly, and she would be asked for autographs. Again, Gwilym thought about how good she was and how she could become a well-known jazz musician if she had a little help. Was he the one to give her that help? An even more important question to ask was did she want that? Did she want to be a wildly successful, well-known jazz pianist? He wished he knew her better.

The second set was calmer. The crowd in the bar seemed to be more into the music. Gwilym definitely was overcome by it. He sat back, nursed his beer, and let the music take him away.

Finally, midnight came, Nina's group, Take Four, began playing "Round Midnight," the classic Thelonious Monk jazz tune, as the crowd began to drift out of the club and onto the street. After a while, Nina joined Gwilym, and they left the club together. Most of the crowd had moved toward the north on Fourth Avenue. Nina spotted Li first. He was standing on the opposite corner with a lovely young woman, his arm around her. Li saw Nina and Gwilym and waved. They both returned the wave.

Suddenly a man dressed all in black and wearing a mask appeared from a dark alley close by that opened on the street. He had what appeared to be a spray can in one hand. The man roughly pushed Li down, kicked Li in the head and chest, then pushed Li onto his stomach. The man began spraying something onto Li's back. Gwilym could see that the can held paint. The girl who had been standing with Li screamed and attempted to push the man away, but he shoved her hard to the pavement. Then he pulled out a gun and shot Li in his right shoulder. The entire interaction took about twenty seconds.

"Two down!" Gwilym heard the man yell.

A couple of people nearby began screaming, but just as quickly, they quieted when the man pointed his gun at them. Then the few people still on the street began running in the opposite direction.

Gwilym pulled Nina behind him. "Go back into the club," he said. "Call the police and call for an ambulance." Nina complied. Gwilym followed her to make sure she was safe, then he turned back to see if he could bring the man down without getting shot himself. But the man had already escaped. As quickly as he had appeared, he now disappeared into the night. He was the same man who had followed Nina home that night and the same man who had shot Vic Davis. Gwilym was dead sure of that. Same size, same movements, same voice.

Gwilym quickly went to Li's side. Li had passed out, but he was breathing, blood seeping from the gunshot wound in his shoulder. He regained consciousness almost immediately. Gwilym could see painted on the back of Li's black leather jacket the numeral two, 2, with a downward-pointing arrow following it. "Two Down."

Gwilym spoke directly to Li in a calm voice. "Li, we've called the cops. We'll get you an ambulance."

Li groaned. "My girl. My girl. Is she okay?"

"Yes, probably bruised, but she's not seriously hurt. I hear the cops and an ambulance coming."

The young woman he'd been with was crawling toward Li on her hands and knees. She was crying. "I tried to stop him," she cried. Gwilym could see that Li's bleeding had stopped. The sirens were coming closer.

Li's girlfriend was sobbing and holding Li's hand now. "I'm okay. I'm okay," Li whispered to her.

Nina had exited the jazz club and had run to Gwilym's side. "Is Li all right?"

Gwilym turned to her. She had a terrified look on her face. She grasped his hand.

"That scumbag shot Li in the shoulder. It doesn't seem too bad, not as bad as Vic," Gwilym answered. "He's conscious, and he's stopped bleeding."

"The ambulance is coming," Nina responded. The sound of sirens pierced the night.

For the next half hour, the scene was eerily like the scene at Vic's shooting. Gwilym and Nina answered police questions and gave the cops their contact information. Li's girlfriend went with him in the ambulance to the hospital.

Gwilym and Nina went to stand under a street light in front of the jazz club's front door.

"Look, Nina. It's late. We need to go back to your place, but I don't want to be exposed walking down dark streets. I'm going to call a taxi." She nodded in agreement. He pulled a phone from his pocket.

Suddenly a taxi appeared from nowhere and came slowly up Fourth Avenue toward them, appearing as if the driver were cruising, looking for a customer. Gwilym took a step forward and raised his hand. The taxi pulled over to the curb and stopped. Gwilym leaned down to take a look at the driver. An older man with a Zapata-style mustache rolled down the window.

"Need a ride?"

"Yes, we only need to go a few blocks."

The taxi driver gestured to the back seat of the taxi.

Gwilym opened the back passenger door. He helped Nina in first, but instead of looking at her, he looked around to see if they were being approached. He could see no one nearby. He climbed in and sat next to Nina, and he gave the taxi driver the address for Nina's apartment building.

The taxi driver pulled away from the curb. At the end of the block, he turned right, drove for two blocks, then halfway into the next block. They were on a street that was only a block north of Casa Pacifica. The street was dark. Gwilym could see only small houses, very few with porch lights on, and no businesses. No one was around.

Gwilym felt alarm surge through his body. Something wasn't right. He could feel it.

Before he could say anything, the taxi driver had opened his driver's side window. The shooter, the masked man who had shot Li only an hour before, appeared from nowhere. He reached out and put something in the taxi driver's extended hand. He pulled his gun out and growled to Nina, "Get out, Nina!" He waved the gun at Gwilym and said, "You, too. Out!"

Gwilym opened the back seat door and exited. He didn't want the gunman to shoot them in the taxi. Too easy. Perhaps he could stall for time.

"What do you want?" Gwilym said, in as calm a voice as he could manage.

"I want you *both* out of the taxi." Again, he waved his gun.

Nina followed Gwilym out. He pulled her behind him, hoping that his taller, broader body would protect her. The taxi driver took off and now it was just the three of them standing in the dark street.

Suddenly and with no warning, Nina took off running to the south. The two men stood there stunned for a couple of seconds, then both immediately began running after her. The gunman was ahead of Gwilym by only a few feet. Nina dodged a couple of cars parked next to the curb, then she jumped up onto a small adobe wall in front of a house. She disappeared behind some oleander bushes in the dark yard.

By this time, Gwilym had caught up with the gunman. He reached out and smashed the man's back with his fists. The man fell to his knees. The impact of the fall caused him to lose his grip on the gun in his hand. The gun skittered noisily across the street pavement and disappeared into the shadows. Gwilym kicked him again roughly in the back, then in the head.

Gwilym stood over the man who was groaning now. Gwilym kicked him again. Suddenly Nina appeared from the dark, grabbed Gwilym's hand, and said, "Come on, let's run."

They began running. Gwilym looked back only once. He could see the gunman pulling himself to his feet. In only a few minutes, Nina and Gwilym were back at the Casa Pacifica apartments. Nina unlocked the entrance door, then ran up the stairs with Gwilym right behind her. She unlocked her door, they went in, and she locked the door behind her.

"Let's not turn on the lights," Nina whispered.

Immediately Gwilym went to stand at the large window facing south in Nina's living room. He peered into the street. Nothing. He turned to Nina and said, "I think we lost him."

"That's because you kicked the shit out of him." She began giggling. The giggles quickly turned into sobs.

Gwilym pulled her into his arms. He held her close as she sobbed. "We're okay. We're okay. We got away from him." He held Nina for a long time, long after she'd stopped crying.

7 The Jazz Game

Tuesday began like any other day except for the workmen who were busy renovating the apartment that would be Zoey Corban's. They were already making noise when Logan woke up Charlie, fed him the last of the frittatta, and made sure Charlie brushed his teeth. Off they went, leaving the workers to their job. He hugged Charlie just before his son went into his kindergarten class.

After Logan had walked Charlie to school, he ran home. It wasn't much of a run, only a few blocks, but it was better than nothing. He'd been sitting around on his butt with his nose in a book for too long. He hadn't been getting any regular exercise so he was thinking seriously of joining a health club in the neighborhood. Lift weights, run on a treadmill, all that stuff. He wanted to look like an adult man, not a skinny, wimpy academic type who sat around and read philosophy books all day. Yeah. Take care of his body. Build some muscles. Eat better. Or maybe just eat regularly. He made sure Charlie ate good food and enough of it. But Logan was lackadaisical about food, and about everything else, too, when it came to taking care of himself. It was time for him to think about his health. Feel better. Look better. Yeah.

At home again, he showered, ate a Mozzarella cheese stick and some roasted almonds, then made a pot of coffee. He took his second cup of coffee outside and sat in the winter sun again. Only a few minutes later, Gwilym joined him.

"Hey, Gwilym," Logan said, "want a cup of coffee?"

"No, I made some already. I spent the night here with Nina. She's still asleep."

Logan grinned. "Good to hear. Nina is a sweetheart, and she needs a good man."

"Thanks, but it wasn't like that. I have a story to tell you."

Logan could see that Gwilym was frowning. "Uh oh. What happened?"

Gwilym gave Logan a quick recounting of Li joining them as they walked to Fourth Avenue, their dinner together, and the set at the jazz club. He went into some detail about Li being shot, the cops and ambulance coming, and the numeral two plus a down arrow spray painted on Li's leather jacket.

"That's bad," Logan said. "Li is okay?"

"Yeah, I called the hospital this morning. His girl is bringing him home late this afternoon or early this evening."

Logan frowned. "The shooter used the phrase 'two down'? So it has to be the same guy who shot Vic."

"Yes, definitely. Same size, some voice, same action with the gun. Then things got even worse."

Logan grimaced.

"I told Nina we needed to get a taxi so we wouldn't have to walk home. That guy with the gun was still out there, and, obviously, I didn't want him following us. Before I had a chance to call, a taxi showed up."

"That was convenient. A set up?"

"Yeah. I didn't think about that at the time, unfortunately. We got in the taxi, and the driver took us only a few blocks to the darkest part of this neighborhood. The gunman showed up and handed the driver something."

"You think it was a payoff?"

"Most likely. We were ordered to get out. We did, and the taxi driver drove away. All of a sudden, Nina took off running, jumped into the yard of a neighborhood house, and hid in the dark. The gunman and I followed her, running at top speed. I caught up with him before he could get to Nina, and I knocked him down and kicked him a few times. He lost control of the gun, and before he could get on his feet again, Nina appeared. She grabbed my hand, and she and I ran full speed back to her apartment."

Logan shook his head in dismay. "You'd better call the cops about this for sure."

"Yes, I'm waiting for Nina to wake up. She was very upset last night. I want to give her a chance to be fully awake and ready to re-live this for the police."

Logan was quiet for a moment. Finally he said, "Li and Nina live in the same apartment building, but Vic doesn't live here. And Li isn't in their jazz group. What's the connection?"

"I think I can explain that. You know what Li looks like. Think about his mustache and beard, a goatee. Also his long, dark hair pulled back."

Logan nodded.

"Have you ever seen Nina's drummer, Santiago Garza?"

"Not in a while. He doesn't usually come around here, and I don't go to clubs late at night."

Gwilym pulled his phone out of his pocket. "Here's a photo of the members of Nina's group." He handed the phone to Logan.

"Oh, crap. I didn't realize that Li and Santiago look so much alike. Same build, both very dark hair pulled back into a knot on the back of their heads, both with a goatee and mustache. One Chinese American. The other Mexican American with a more Native look." He looked at

Gwilym and shook his head. "The gunman mixed them up."

"That's what I think. He thought he was targeting Nina's band mate, Santiago, but instead he assaulted a Chinese American chef named Li who happens to live in the same building as Nina."

"Okay. So we can conclude that the target is Take Four, Nina's band."

Gwilym nodded. "That's exactly what I think. One down was Vic, two down was Santiago, or so the gunman thought. He went after Nina next. The fourth member of the group is Zeke Overton."

"Is he picking them off one-by-one and saving the best for last? Is Zeke special somehow?"

Gwilym shook his head. "Maybe, but I don't really think we can say that for sure. Going after Nina was probably opportunistic. It's possible the gunman hadn't expected to see her and decided to act when she was available to him."

"In any case, we need to warn both Santiago and Zeke Overton. And Nina is still a target." On top of this, Logan did not like the idea of some maniac with a gun show-ing up at the apartments where his boy Charlie lived and played. Logan felt tension all over his body.

"I'll talk to Nina about warning Zeke. I showed her the photo of Santiago and asked her if she could see the resemblance between him and Li. She agreed. And I'm staying with her until we get all this figured out. He could really hurt her, and I'm not going to allow that."

"Did you talk to Nina anymore about this? Does she have any idea why she and the others might be a target? Any idea who this guy is?"

"No. She says she's clueless. And the not-knowing is very stressful for her."

"I get that," Logan said. "I'm so sorry both of you are going through this."

"Yeah, me, too. So you want to help us figure out what is going on? You're a long-time Tucsonan so I think you'll have a better idea of how to start looking into this. I'm an outsider. I don't know where to begin."

"Of course, I'll help as best I can. I'll do some research and see if I can figure out which of the four band members has some history that might have led to this. Who has a grudge against whom? Is there a conflict over money? Or some kind of competition? Who wants the band to stop performing and why? Or is there some other goal?"

"Right. We don't know enough right now except that the targets are the Take Four members."

Just at that moment, Nina appeared. She walked slowly down the back steps toward them. Her face was pale, and she looked exhausted.

"Hey, Nina," Logan's voice was gentle. "Gwilym told me what happened."

Nina shook her head. "I'm so sorry. I must have done something wrong."

"Not your fault, Nina." Gwilym said firmly. "Stop blaming yourself."

"We'll figure it out," Logan said. "But first you must call Zeke and Santiago and warn them."

Nina nodded. "We're not scheduled to play tonight. I'll call them now."

"I'll go up with you and make you some breakfast," Gwilym said. "And we'll call the cops and report this."

Nina's laugh was sardonic. "The cops are going to be sick of me. This is the third time they've had to talk to me in three days."

"Good," Gwilym said. "That means that they will take all this very seriously."

"I'm going to go get my laptop and come back here. I'm going to do some research," Logan said. "I'll direct the cops to your apartment, Nina."

She nodded. "I'm so glad you two are here. I wouldn't know what to do if I were alone now."

"You are not alone," Gwilym said. "Come on. I'll get you some coffee. What do you want for breakfast? Maybe you can show me how to make some of that Sonoran cuisine. So delicious. Some egg dish maybe? How about that, sweetheart?" He put his arm around Nina and led her to the back steps. He looked back at Logan and nodded, a serious look on his face.

Logan returned the nod. He went in, retrieved his laptop, and sat down at the table, ready to begin searching for anything and everything he could find about the Take Four band members. He opened a special document to collect links and notes. He began right away.

~~~

Nina and Gwilym went back to her apartment. "I'll make you something simple, Nina."

"You don't have to make breakfast. I'm not really hungry."

"You're too stressed now. But you need to eat something. Later. I'm going to really cook for you. An Indian meal. My mom taught me how to make a delicious curry. You'll like that."

They ate breakfast, then Gwilym called the police, explained the situation and requested a police officer to visit. Nina called both Santiago and Zeke, told them what happened the night before, and warned them to watch their backs. "We're trying to figure out why our group is being targeted," she told them. "Until we figure out who this nutcase is, each of us has to be really careful and stay safe."

As Nina spoke, Gwilym watched her. She was so beautiful and so sweet and sexy, too. He knew that his feelings for her were growing by the minute. Beautiful and sweet, but she also was very stressed. He wanted to do something that would make her forget all her troubles for a little while, to be relieved of the stress and anxiety, to smile again, maybe even laugh.

They went to the sofa near the window overlooking the street. They were quiet for a while, holding hands.

"I think you need a distraction," Gwilym said. "Something that will take so much of your attention that you'll forget all this other unpleasantness."

"That's sweet of you, but I don't think it's going to be easy to distract me."

"We'll see." Gwilym smiled. "How about if we play a game?"

"A game? What kind of game?"

"The Jazz Game. I'll give you the name of a jazz musician. Or jazz group. You tell me where the person or group is from, and if it's an individual, which instrument he or she plays."

Nina shook her head, smiling. "You're confused. I'm the jazz musician. I should be asking you these questions."

"I don't think so, Nina Simone Perry. I know more about jazz than you do." He tilted his head back, a superior look on his face.

Nina's eyebrows went up. She grinned. "Okay, smarty pants. Let's see who knows the most. Ask me a question."

"First question. Bill Evans."

"Oh, that's easy. American, piano."

Gwilym leaned forward and kissed her on the cheek.

"That's your reward for giving me a correct answer," he said.

"Oh, jeez. Thanks so much for a peck on the cheek."

Gwilym chuckled. "Manu Katche."

"French. Plays percussion."

"Very good." He kissed her on her cheek again.

"Enrico Pieranunzi."

"Italian. Piano."

Another peck on the cheek.

"Diana Krall."

"Canadian. Piano. Also a vocalist."

Another peck.

"Tord Gustavsen."

Nina frowned. "Piano. Norwegian?" She paused. "Yes, Norwegian."

She got another peck on the cheek. She sighed.

"Till Bronner."

"Trumpet." Nina paused. "I'm not sure. Sweden? No. Germany. Definitely Germany."

Another peck.

"Eliana Elias."

"Brazilian. Piano. Vocalist."

After he kissed her on the cheek, Gwilym smiled. "I'm being too easy on you. The next question will be more difficult."

"Bring it on," Nina giggled.

This is working, Gwilym said to himself. She's laughing.

"Modern Jazz Quartet."

"That's easy. American. John Lewis was the pianist. He passed away a few years ago."

Another peck.

"Ponta Box."

Nina's face fell. She frowned. After a long moment, she said, "Never heard of Ponta Box."

"Oh, too bad. Turns out you don't know everything, do you, Miss Smarty Pants? Ponta Box was a Japanese jazz group led by Suichi Murakami."

Nina shook her head. "And I guess that means I don't even get that sad little peck you call a kiss."

"On the contrary. You get a pity kiss."

"A pity kiss?" Nina grinned. "What's a pity kiss?"

"I show my pity for your obvious ignorance." He leaned forward, put his arms around her, pulled her close, and touched his lips to hers. What started as soft and gentle quickly transformed into a hungry, passionate kiss, then another, and another.

"That's a pity kiss." Gwilym pulled back, smiling.

Nina sighed, her eyes on his. "My goodness. A pity kiss."

"Okay. Let's keep going. Keith Jarrett."

"Keith Jarrett," Nina repeated. She looked at him with a smile on her face. "Never heard of Keith Jarrett." She batted her eye lashes.

Gwilym chuckled. "The first time I met you, I told you that your playing sounded a lot like Keith Jarrett. You thanked me, and you said that Keith Jarrett is one of your favorites. I think you definitely know who Keith Jarrett is."

Nina shook her head no. "Never heard of Keith Jarrett. So does this mean I get a pity kiss?"

"Yes, you get a pity kiss because you are so pitiful." The kisses this time were increasingly intense. She clung to Gwilym, her arms around his neck, as his hands pulled her closer and roamed over her body.

Suddenly there was a loud knock on the door.

"That's probably the police," Gwilym said.

"Oh, bad timing," Nina said. "I was really enjoying being so pitiful."

~~~

Logan was sitting outside again, diligently searching the internet on his laptop when the cop showed up. He was the same police officer that had interviewed Gwilym, Nina and him at Vic's shooting. His name tag said Officer J. Alvarez. Logan stood up and held out his hand.

"Office Alvarez, good to see you again. Thanks for coming. You spoke with me when you investigated the assault on Vic Davis."

"Yes, I remember you. You've had another incident."

"Not me. The other two you spoke to that day are the ones you want to talk to." Logan directed Officer Alvarez to Nina's upstairs apartment.

As soon as Alvarez headed upstairs, Logan went back to work. He made a separate file for all four of the musicians in Take Four, which included Nina, Santiago on drums, Zeke on sax, and Vic on bass. He'd already made a list of things to look for. Any legal problems. Close relatives with legal problems. Any items in the news that connected the band member with any kind of problem or conflict. He looked for connections to individuals who might have a grudge against one of the musicians or the entire group, someone who wanted revenge for some insult or perceived slight, or someone who had a reason to see Take Four put out of business. The list of possibilities was long. He tried to keep an open mind about any connections.

After about half an hour, Alvarez reappeared. "Mr. Reid, I'd like to remind you that if you have another incident with the shooter, call me immediately. This man is dangerous, and we need to get him off the streets as soon as possible."

"Yes, definitely, Officer Alvarez. I'm trying to find any connection now that might give us a clue. It's bothering us that this guy disappears so quickly."

"Bothers me, too. Makes me wonder if he lives in this area and knows his way around. That may be why. We're looking for him now. Also we're going to try to find that taxi driver they encountered last night."

Logan nodded.

"Okay," the police officer said. "Contact me directly if you have any trouble or if you find useful information. Here's my number." He handed Logan a card.

It was early afternoon when Gwilym came downstairs. Logan was searching on his computer.

"Have you found anything?" Gwilym asked.

"Maybe. Seems like everyone in the group except Vic has had some kind of conflict with someone or another. Santiago has family members who have been arrested, usually for smuggling people or drugs. But Santiago doesn't have an arrest record as far as I can tell. Zeke, I don't know, there's something about his dad getting sued by a corporate firm the dad used to work for. Zeke himself has been arrested a couple of times. Looks like he was an older wild-ass teenager who shoplifted and sold drugs."

"And Nina?"

"No indication that she's ever been in trouble. Her dad had a legal battle with someone who used to be his partner. I'm not exactly sure what the issue was. It seemed to be about control over original tunes they recorded together. Her dad and the partner both claimed to be the composer or lyricist with full rights. Ownership meant control of income. Kind of like control over who wrote a book and who gets income from sales."

They both looked up when Frida Villarreal skipped down the back steps and waved to Logan and Gwilym. "Hi, guys. Whatcha doing?"

Gwilym remembered Frida from the group's Sunday dinner. She was the one who said she spent most of her time engaged in various social and political causes.

"I'm hanging out here hoping to keep Nina safe," Gwilym said.

"And I'm trying to find out any information I can to identify this butt head who likes to shoot people," Logan answered.

"Yeah, I heard about Li getting shot. I think I can help you get more info. I have a friend." She wiggled her eyebrows.

Logan smiled. "Legally-acquired information, Frida." They all laughed.

"Yeah. Whatever. His name is Frankie Miranda. Actually he's the cousin of my ex-husband. Frankie is much nicer than my ex. He's a computer geek, and he's training to become a private investigator. I bet he could help you. Look for Valdez Investigations on the web. You can contact him that way. Tell him I sent you. He'll probably do it for free if it's just computer searches."

Logan looked up the website. "I'll do that right away. Thanks, Frida."

"Okay. I'm off. I have a meeting of my collective. Then I go to work this evening. Bye!"

Logan quickly emailed the Contact at Valdez Investigations.

"What's the collective Frida mentioned?" Gwilym asked.

"She and her activist pals are planning some kind of demonstration. I think it's about wages for a local workers' union. Members all work for the same grocery store chain. I'm sure she'd be very happy to tell you all about it and invite you to participate in the demonstration, too." He closed his laptop. "It's almost time for me to pick up

Charlie from kindergarten. So you're sticking around here?"

"Yeah. I just don't think it's safe for Nina to be all alone."

"That's good. A relief really." Logan stood and headed for his own apartment. "I'm going to get a bite to eat and then go get Charlie. See you later this afternoon."

Gwilym nodded and headed back to Nina's apartment.

~~~

Later that afternoon, Charlie and Logan were sitting outdoors in the winter sun again when Nina and Gwilym appeared. Charlie looked up at Nina. "I'm doing my homework. My daddy is helping me. I'm on the last problem."

"Beginning arithmetic," Logan said.

Just at that moment, Zoey Corban came walking briskly up the walk to the apartment building.

"Hello everyone!" she called out cheerfully. She waved, and everyone waved back except for Charlie. When he saw her, he jumped up, cried out "Zoey!" He ran to meet her and threw his arms around her waist in a tight hug. Zoey hugged him back. Logan was surprised. He couldn't remember ever seeing Charlie being so affectionate with someone he barely knew.

"I'm on my way to soccer practice so I thought I'd come by and see how the apartment renovations are going."

Logan stood. "Come on and I'll show you." He and Charlie entered the back door, went into the interior hallway, and opened the door to the apartment that would be Zoey's.

"Wow. You've done a lot in such a short time," Zoey said. Charlie put his hand in hers as she walked through the apartment.

"Yes, but there's still more to do," Logan said. "The workman will be back here again tomorrow. I'm pretty sure we'll be done by this weekend."

They went back outside.

"The apartment looks great," Zoey told Nina.

"I'll be glad when you get moved in." Nina smiled. "We can visit more often."

Charlie spoke up. "Zoey, what do you eat for breakfast?"

Zoey was surprised at Charlie's question. She looked over at Logan. He was biting his lower lip, trying not to laugh.

"Well, usually I make a smoothie with vanilla yogurt and some fruit juice and fruit mixed in. Like blueberries or bananas. Blueberries are my favorite. And if I'm in a hurry, I just eat a Mozzarella cheese stick and some roasted almonds."

Logan's eyebrows went up.

"What about that famous cereal for kids with the little circle rings in different colors?" Charlie asked.

Zoey looked at Logan again. He was making a face.

"No. I don't eat that kind of thing. Too much sugar. I think it's gross. What did you eat for breakfast today?"

"I had some frittata and a glass of milk."

"Frittata! Oh, lucky you! I love frittata!"

Charlie pointed to Logan. "My daddy made it!"

"Lucky you to have daddy that makes such a delicious breakfast." Zoey grinned at Logan.

"Charlie, Zoey has given us a good idea about smoothies. I'll make you a yogurt smoothie soon with your favorite fruit," Logan said.

"A banana!" Charlie grinned.

"I have to go now. See you later!" Zoey waved good bye and took off walking briskly.

"Hurry and move in," Charlie called to her. She waved again.

"Come on, Charlie. Let's go in and see about some supper." Logan picked up the homework papers, and they headed into their apartment.

Nina and Gwilym were still sitting on the back porch.

"You're right about that," Gwilym said.

"Right about what?"

"Logan turns pink when he looks at Zoey."

Nina giggled. "Definitely pink."

"I think Logan and Zoey are both kind of shy," Gwilym said.

"Yes, I'm going to help them with that." Nina took Gwilym's hand, and they went back inside.

8 FRANKIE

Gwilym woke early the next morning. He was sleeping on Nina's couch again. He sighed, going over their conversation from last evening.

Nina had started the conversation by asking him if he wanted to play the Jazz Game again.

He'd reached out and taken her hand in his. "Nina, it's like this. I'm crazy about you. I know we haven't known each other for very long, but I'm pretty sure I'm falling in love with you. However, right now we're in a weird, very high-stress situation. I don't want to pull you into something with me because of this crazy situation, and then later, you regret it."

"And you think the Jazz Game would be difficult for us?" she asked softly.

Gwilym kissed her hand. "I think you'll want more than pity kisses. That would be really hard on me because I want more than pity kisses, too. I can't tell you how much I desire you. It would be so hard for me to resist going to the next step." He frowned. "But there's the matter of keeping watch. I want you to be safe. That comes first. Your safety. If you and I…." He hesitated. "I won't be able to keep watch if we distract ourselves like that."

Nina sighed. She was quiet for a few minutes then finally she said, "Okay. What you say makes sense. And you're right about those pity kisses. I've fallen for you, too, and I want you. I want to make love with you. So let's wait until this bad stuff is over. I can wait."

"I hope you will wait. I desperately hope you will wait."

She smiled. "I will. I will wait. And when all this is over, I expect a very huge dose of pity from you, Gwilym Sanjay Havard. Hours and hours of pity. Days of pity. In my bed pity."

He groaned. "Oh god."

She laughed and kissed him. "Then we'll be free to follow the jazz lines."

Gwilym grinned. "Yes, follow the jazz lines."

Nina went to her bedroom, and Gwilym slept on the couch.

Now it was time to start a new day. Gwilym went to the kitchen to make some coffee. Fifteen minutes later, he was downstairs. He knocked on Logan's door.

"Come in," Logan said. He was at his dining table looking at his computer.

"Have you found anything?" Gwilym asked.

"Nothing new. But I emailed and then talked to Frankie Miranda. He said because he works for a private investigator, he has access to sources of information that the general public can't access. I just got a text from him. He's supposed to show up here in fifteen or twenty minutes. He said he's found quite a bit of info."

"That's good news. I've been thinking. This has to be something personal. Someone wants to make it impossible for Take Four to play together."

"Or separately. Getting shot makes it hard to play your instrument in or out of a group," Logan said.

"Yeah. The shooter wants to put an end to the group and to the musicians, too. They won't be able to easily regroup and continue playing."

"But I can't help but think that there has to be some-one in the group who is the real target. The fact that the shooter confused Li and Santiago indicates that they were just in the way."

"So we have to figure out who is the target and why," Gwilym said.

"Yeah, that's what I think."

There was a soft knock on the door. Logan went to open it. He was surprised to find a man there who didn't look anything like what he thought a private investigator would look like.

"Hi. I'm Frankie Miranda."

"I'm Logan Reid. Come on in. This is Gwilym Havard. He's visiting here, and he's staying with Nina Perry who lives upstairs."

Frankie sat down at Logan's dining room table and pulled out his laptop from a beat up briefcase he was carrying.

Logan looked him over. Frankie Miranda was a small man, maybe five feet six inches at most. He was dressed in black denim pants, a gray t-shirt, and a black hoodie. He had a black Fedora hat on his head. When he took off his hoodie, Logan could see that his hands, his arms, and his neck were covered in tattoos. His ears were gauged with silver rings lining the openings in his ear lobes. Not your typical private investigator, Logan thought. But then Logan realized his idea about private investigators came from television shows, not real life.

Logan and Gwilym started talking at once. Gwilym stopped, and Logan took over. "We want to tell you how much we appreciate your doing this. We're kind of at a loss."

Frankie nodded. "No problem. Actually this is a good time. I'm a student at the university, and we're between semesters so I have some free time. My boss is on a trip, and we don't have any active investigations right now."

"Your boss?" Gwilym asked.

"Yeah, Letty Valdez. She's a licensed private investigator. She's training me to get my PI license. My specialty is computer forensics."

"Oh." Logan wasn't sure what to say. "Is she working on a case outside of Tucson?"

"No. She got married. Her new husband took her on a honeymoon." Frankie laughed. "Letty calls it a trip. Dan calls it a honeymoon because he's the romantic one. Letty is always kind of serious. She goes on trips, not honeymoons." He laughed again.

"Where did they go?" Gwilym asked.

"Oh, some island in the Caribbean. Letty sent me a postcard from St. Maarten. I had to look it up on the map because I'd never heard of it. Letty wrote a note on the card. She said there was water everywhere." Frankie laughed. "I guess so. St. Maarten is an island in the ocean so there would be water everywhere. Kind of a weird for a desert rat, I guess. Her husband Dan took her there so he could teach Letty how to surf." He laughed again. "I'd like to see that. Letty Valdez on a surfboard."

"Why is that amusing?" Logan asked.

"Letty is six feet tall, a Mexican American-Native American. Tohono O'odham. Serious. Doesn't smile much. She's a martial arts expert, and she carries a gun on her a lot of the time." Frankie laughed. "It's just kind of hard to imagine her on a surfboard."

Logan and Gwilym didn't know what to say. But both of them were very curious now. They both hoped to meet this Letty Valdez someday.

Frankie added, "But let me be clear. Letty is the best. I respect her so much. She gave me a chance for a new life.

I was clerking in a grocery store in Nogales, and now I'm training to be a private investigator. So if Letty wants to surf, I'm totally okay with that."

Logan and Gwilym nodded.

"Okay. Let's get started," Frankie said.

"Fine. Where do we start?" Logan asked.

"Let's look at Vic Davis. He's the easiest one to dismiss. Everything about him is pretty open and clear. He's the bass player in the Take Four jazz group, learned to play bass in high school, works part time at a convenience store, has a wife and kids, and he's an elder in the Mt. Calvary Baptist Church. It's the oldest African American church in Tucson. He also plays in a musical group at the church. You know, his church musical group is there to accompany the choir singing hymns."

"So everything seems to be fine with him? No past arrests? No jealous girlfriends? No drug dealing on the side?" Gwilym asked.

"Nope. He's a good guy, very upfront, someone you'd go to if you needed a free meal or a ride to the doctor. From everything I found about him, Vic Davis is highly respected."

"How about the others in the group?" Logan asked.

"That's where things get a lot more interesting. We can access several online databases just for investigators. I found quite a bit more information. I have an idea about who is the target, but I want to review the information first."

"Okay." Both Logan and Gwilym nodded their heads in agreement.

"First," Frankie began, "let's look at Santiago Garza. He has family on both sides of the border, primarily in the Nogales area. Most of the family members on both sides are just regular citizens. Many of the women are shopkeepers, both in the business district and in the big tourist market. A couple of the men are factory workers, one is a mechanic. One of the men owns and operates a restaurant. His wife works there, too. For the most part, they just seem like regular folk."

Frankie looked up at them. Both Logan and Gwilym were paying close attention.

"However," Frankie grinned, "things get more interesting when we look at Santiago's uncles. Santiago's father is one of four brothers in this branch of the family. He came over to the U.S. side of the line years ago and married a Mexican American. He has citizenship now. But let's look at one of the brothers that stayed on the Mexican side. His name is Felix Garza."

"He's doing something illegal?" Logan asked.

"Felix works as a car mechanic. But for a long time, he had a side gig going as a coyote."

Gwilym raised his eyebrows. "A coyote? I thought that was an animal, kind of like a wolf or dog, that lives in western North America. We have them in British Columbia, too, although I think coyotes are more common here."

Logan explained: "In this case, 'coyote' is a slang term for someone who smuggles people across the border. For a fee, of course."

"Ah," Gwilym responded. "I see."

"Yes, a very good fee," Logan responded. "At least two thousand dollars per person, and often double that. Or even more."

"Wow. And definitely illegal." Gwilym was learning something new.

Frankie nodded. "So Felix had a pretty successful business going. Word is that he tried to expand his business by recruiting teenage boys to drive the illegals across. The teens can be Mexicans, but usually they are U.S. citizens. They typically drive a van packed with illegals."

"Why teenagers?" Gwilym asked.

"If they are under eighteen years old and get caught by the authorities, they are usually released because they are minors," Frankie continued. "They get paid several hundred dollars for bringing a group across."

"I read somewhere," Logan interjected, "that these teens are often told that if the Border Patrol tries to stop them, they should take off driving as fast as possible because Border Patrol won't chase them."

"Yeah, but that's not correct," Frankie said. "BP will come after them. There have been several high-speed chases that have ended in crashes and the deaths of both the immigrants and the teen drivers."

Gwilym shook his head.

"Okay," Frankie continued. "So Felix recruited his nephew Santiago to bring a van across. Santiago was seventeen and a student at one of the high schools in Tucson. He was already a musician playing percussion in a rock band. He wanted to buy a better drum set so he agreed to bring the van across so he could make some extra money. Unfortunately, the van was spotted by Border Patrol, Santiago took off driving really fast, and Border Patrol followed close behind. Santiago ended up losing control and crashing the van. He and a couple of the illegal immigrants spent time in the hospital. All the illegals were deported. On top of that, Felix refused to pay Santiago, and he refused to give the deported illegals a refund."

Gwilym snorted.

"We have a good slang word in Mexican Spanish for dudes like Felix. That's *pendejo.*" Frankie grinned.

"I can imagine what that means," Gwilym said.

"Santiago's parents were furious. But then they did something really smart," Frankie continued. "They bought him a new drum set, got music lessons for him, and connected him to the Tucson Jazz Institute. It's a local organization devoted to creating opportunities for young musicians."

"Wow! That was *very* smart!" Gwilym grinned.

"Of course, they made it clear that if he screwed up again, they would kick him out of the house and be done with him. Santiago decided that music was a better career option than smuggling illegal immigrants." Frankie sat back and crossed his arms in front of him. He was enjoying this.

"You think there might be a connection to this shooter we're dealing with now?" Logan asked.

"Maybe. Maybe, but unlikely. Felix is kind of an outcast now in the family. He may harbor a grudge against Santiago or against his brother, Santiago's father. Felix had to shut down his illegal operations, and he ended up losing money because one of the cartels moved into his territory and took over the smuggling biz. Felix may still be angry and blame Santiago for all the bad times he's experiencing now."

"Enough to try to kill Santiago and possibly his band members, too? Several years have passed," Logan added.

"You can't really overestimate how some people will hold a grudge for a long time and try eventually to get revenge. But, it does seem unlikely. Also based on your description, the shooter can't be Felix. He's in his fifties now and is quite chubby. Too many taquitos, I'd say."

Gwilym nodded. "The shooter is a little on the thin side, not as tall as me or Logan. And the way he moves suggests he's fairly young."

"Felix could have hired the shooter," Logan pointed out.

"True. It's a possibility. I just don't think it's likely," Frankie said.

"Let's move on then," Logan said. "Who is next?"

"Zeke Overton. Jazz sax in the Take Four group." Frankie looked at his computer screen and clicked on his mouse. "Zeke comes from an affluent white family that lives in the Catalina Foothills. His father worked for a big corporation that is headquartered back East. The father heads the local office, and the mom stays home and tells the maids what to do. Zeke is the only child. The family has quite a bit of money so Zeke always got whatever he wanted. But my guess is that the parents didn't pay much attention to Zeke when he was growing up."

Logan thought about Charlie. He vowed to himself to never be that kind of parent. Charlie would always know how much he was loved. Always.

"I say that because Zeke managed to get himself into a lot of trouble when he was a teen. Despite the family being affluent and despite the fact that Zeke could have whatever he wanted, he got caught more than once shop lifting. And he also got caught selling some drugs to kids at school. Weed mainly."

"And I bet he got off," Logan said.

"Yep. Rich daddy hires a top notch lawyer. Son gets probation."

"He's quite an accomplished jazz saxophonist. How did that happen?" Gwilym asked.

"His high school music teacher took an interest in Zeke and turned him onto jazz."

"We should value our teachers more," said Logan.

"So you don't think Zeke has anything to do with the shooter?" Gwilym asked.

"No," Frankie said. "There's no obvious reason to be bringing down Zeke and his group. Or none that I have been able to determine."

"Here's some good news," Gwilym said. "Nina told me last night that her percussionist Santiago decided to take a trip to visit relatives in Oaxaca, and the sax player, Zeke, took off for Europe to do a jazz fest tour."

"I guess they decided things were a little too hot for them here. So Take Four is disbanded now," Logan said, "or maybe just on hold?"

"Can't say what will happen," Gwilym said. "Too bad it came to this, but at least Santiago and Zeke won't be targets anymore. And if that shooter comes after Nina, he'll have to deal with me first."

"So let's move on to Nina,"Logan said. "What did you find about her?"

"That's where things get *really* interesting," Frankie said.

"Uh oh." Logan made a face. "What do you mean, 'really interesting'?"

"Nina was born and lived in New York City until she was sixteen. Her dad was a fairly well known jazz musician. He also recorded several albums that are still available. The family moved out here, and Nina finished high school here in Tucson. She's pretty close to finishing her degree now at the University of Arizona."

"We're familiar with this," Logan said. "Nina never has much money. I guess her parents can't really help her."

"Her dad, his name is Ted Perry, had a stroke after the family moved here. He can't play anymore so he and his wife live off income from his albums and from the sale of music rights. They really don't have enough extra to support Nina. They are elderly now and live a very simple life."

Gwilym nodded. "So he gets income from other artists who want to record his original compositions?"

"In some cases, yes," Frankie said. "He's even sold the complete rights for individual tunes to publishers, which means once he's paid a chunk of money for a tune, he gets no more income."

"This is kind of like copyright and book publishing?" Logan asked.

"Yes, sort of, but here's the first interesting thing. Nina's dad had a long-term relationship with another musician when he was in New York City, Ralph Reddick. They played and recorded together for years. When Nina's dad sold the rights, he did not share the income with Reddick who claimed to be his partner. Reddick sued Nina's dad, insisting that they should share income from recording rights and album sales, too. Reddick claimed to be the lyricist and claimed that Nina's dad was the composer."

Frankie took a deep breath. "They went to court, and Nina's dad won the case. Ted Perry testified that the musical group was his, he was in charge, and Reddick got paid a salary for years. That is, he testified that Reddick was his paid employee, and that Reddick had not written a note or a lyric in all those years. Several musicians, including a couple of vocalists, testified and backed up Nina's dad. To this day, all the income from the music goes to Nina's dad. Such as it is. Jazz tunes don't make the big bucks that a rock-and-roller makes. That explains why Nina is pretty much on her own when it comes to supporting herself."

"This no doubt caused a great deal of resentment in the so-called partner?" Gwilym asked.

"Right. Then things got way worse. Perry had two kids, a son named Drew, and Nina, his daughter. Reddick had two sons. When Drew Perry was a teenager, he and Reddick's older son, Alex, went out partying. They got really drunk or high, or both. Drew was driving way too fast and lost control of the car. They had a huge crash, and both Drew and Alex were killed."

Logan shook his head. Tragic. The idea of Charlie being a teenage boy scared the hell out of him.

Frankie continued: "These deaths happened not long before the Perry family moved to Tucson. My guess is the Perry family wanted to start a new life here and forget the pain and grief of the past. Fairly recently, Ralph Reddick had a heart attack and died."

"What about the second son?" Logan asked.

"Exactly," Frankie smiled. "Clever of you to think of him. If all this happened to your family, a lost court case, no income, a dead brother and then a dead dad, you might be the kind of person who developed a great deal of resentment, murderous resentment."

"And you would go after Nina, not Nina's dad, but Nina. Stop her from playing, from having a successful career as a jazz musician, and make sure that Nina's dad, Ted Perry, sees all this and suffers because of it." Gwilym shook his head.

"So we need to identify and locate Ethan Reddick."

"Oh, *merde*," Gwilym said, "I just remembered this. When the gunman told us to get out of the taxi, he said, 'Get out, Nina,' and then to me, he just said, 'You, too.'"

"That means he knows Nina," Logan said. "He got Li and Santiago mixed up but not Nina. He knows her."

"Take a look at this photo." Frankie turned his laptop toward them so they could see the screen. "This is Ethan Reddick. Recognize him?"

Logan and Gwilym looked at the young man, mid-twenties, slender, light brown hair, blue-gray eyes staring intently at the camera.

"When I've seen him, he's always been masked," Gwilym said, "but I think I recognize the eyes. I'm going to get Nina and see if she recognizes him."

"Good idea," Logan said. "Also can you email me a copy? I'll forward it to the detective working on this case."

"Consider it done," Frankie said.

Gwilym was already out the door of Logan's apartment. He ran up the stairs, and he returned with Nina in only a couple of minutes.

"Hi, guys," she said as she entered Logan's apartment.

Logan introduced Frankie. Nina didn't blink at eye at his unusual appearance. She smiled and waved.

"We'd like you to take a look at a photo of someone and see if you recognize him," Frankie said.

"Sure." Nina smiled.

Frankie turned the computer screen toward her.

Nina gasped and took a step backward.

"What?" Gwilym asked.

"Yes, I know him. Ethan Reddick is his name. He's a real jerk. He and I went to high school together before I moved out here. He kept asking me to go out with him, and he wouldn't take no for an answer. He was very aggressive. But I had this bad feeling about him. I didn't feel safe around him so I kept saying no." She looked at the others. "We were only sixteen. Why are you showing me his photo?"

Frankie nodded. "Okay, add to the family-linked resentment and a desire for revenge, there's something else, humiliation due to a girl's repeated rejection of him."

Logan looked directly at Nina. "We think he's the shooter."

9 Assault

Nina's eyes filled with tears. Gwilym put his arm around her.

"I'll call the police officer, tell him that I just sent him this photo, and let him know the shooter's name," Logan said.

Gwilym nodded. "I'm taking Nina upstairs. This is a lot to handle all at once." He turned before they left and asked Frankie, "What do we owe you?"

"Nothing," Frankie grinned. "This was fun. Solving mysteries is always a lot of fun for me. I hope it all turns out well for you so please keep me updated. I have to go now. My beautiful Sam is waiting for me."

"Sam?" Logan asked.

"Really Samantha, but she likes to be called Sam." Frankie packed up his computer and said goodbye.

"Thanks again, Frankie," Logan waved goodbye. He turned to his cell phone, retrieved the photo and then forwarded it to Officer Alvarez. Two minutes later, his phone buzzed.

"Hello, Mr. Reid. I just received this photo. You think this is the shooter?" Alvarez asked.

"Almost certain," Logan said. He gave the police officer a brief history of Nina and her family, the lawsuit and the deadly car accident in which the two young men were killed. "Nina identified him as Ethan Reddick." He explained Reddick's relationship to Nina.

"Okay. I'll put out an APB for him. That's an all-points bulletin that will go out to law enforcement, both local and statewide. When he's apprehended, we'll bring him in for questioning. Also we'll start checking security cameras at different businesses in the Iron Horse neighborhood and on Fourth Avenue. We may be able to locate where he's living."

"Anything I can do to help?" Logan asked.

"Not at this point. Just watch your back. You and that other fellow, the Canadian, the two of you can do your best to keep a watch on Nina Perry, too. The shooter will try to get to her. I hope we can get to him first."

They said their goodbyes.

Logan could hear the soft sounds of a piano coming from Nina's apartment upstairs. That's good, he thought to himself. Gwilym is encouraging her to play the piano. Get lost in the music. That's best. Gwilym is definitely a good guy, he decided.

Logan looked at the clock on his wall.

"Oh, god. Never enough time in the day." He grabbed his wallet and shopping bag and headed for the small grocery store about two blocks from his apartment. Thirty minutes later, he was stuffing big cups of vanilla yogurt, fruit juice and blueberries into his fridge. Bananas went into the basket on the dining table. Smoothies. Why hadn't he thought of that? Maybe he could ask Zoey for more ideas about what to feed a five year-old who thinks sugary crap is great to eat.

Logan ate a quick lunch. Melted cheese on toast plus some almonds, a sliced tomato and a handful of the blueberries. He had to admit that he wasn't really into cooking. He only did it because Charlie needed to have decent food and a normal mealtime with his dad. Speaking of, it was time to go pick up Charlie from kindergarten.

By mid-afternoon, Charlie and Logan were sitting outside again in the January sunshine. They were both wearing straw hats.

"I have some homework to do," Charlie said. He pulled some paper and crayons out of his backpack.

"Okay, what's your homework?"

"Today we learned shapes."

"Shapes? What do you mean?"

"Oh, you know. Like square, circle, triangle, rectangle, hexagon, octagon. My favorite is octagon. It has eight sides. I have to draw them. I can decorate them, too. Like make faces on them, and make them different colors."

Logan nodded. "Okay. I'll read my book while you're working on that."

Charlie went to work, head down, concentrating diligently.

A few minutes later, Gwilym appeared. He sat down at the table. "Nina is resting now. This has been pretty traumatic for her."

Logan nodded. "I'm really glad you're here. Nina has really benefited from all your help. By the way, I called Officer Alvarez. He's on the job looking for this nutcase."

A small red car drove up and parked at the curb in front of the apartment house. Zoey Corban exited from the driver's side. When Charlie saw her, he called out, "Zoey!" and he ran to meet her. They exchanged hugs.

"Come and look at my homework," Charlie said, "I'm doing shapes." He took her hand and pulled her toward the big outdoor table. She said hi to Logan and Gwilym and then sat down next to Charlie who explained what he was doing.

"So these are the basic shapes," Zoey said. "Are you allowed to add some more?"

"I don't know." Charlie frowned, then a grin appeared. "Why not? Give me some more shapes, Zoey."

"Okay." She picked up a pencil and began drawing on a sheet of paper. "This is a star shape. It has five points. And this star is called a hexagram. It has six points. See how if you put two triangles together, you can make a hexagram."

"Oh, yeah!" Charlie giggled.

"The six-point star has been important in human history. I'll tell you about that sometime. And here's my favorite shape." She drew a heart.

"I know that one!" Charlie pointed at his dad. "My daddy has a heart! I can hear it when he holds me."

Zoey looked over at Logan. "That's so sweet," She smiled.

Gwilym noticed Logan was turning pink again.

"Charlie, did you know that Zoey is a teacher?" Logan said.

"Do you teach kindergarten?" Charlie asked.

"No. I teach high school biology. Do you know what that is?"

"No. Does it have to do with shapes?"

"Sometimes. The word 'biology' comes from two Greek words. 'Bios' means 'life' and 'logos' means 'study.' So I study life. Things like animals, plants, birds, bugs, anything that is alive. Some living things have interesting shapes."

"I like bugs," Charlie said.

"Ah, an entomologist. That's someone who likes bugs. We can go on a bug hunt sometime." She smiled and wiggled her eyebrows.

"Really! Daddy, can I go on a bug hunt with Zoey?"

"Yes, of course."

Gwilym laughed but not about the bug hunt. Logan was turning a dark pink. He'd tell Nina about this for sure.

"Okay. I'm going to say goodbye now. I'm here to chat with Nina. I haven't had a chance to visit with her in a while. Nice to see you, Charlie."

"Bye, Zoey." He muttered "bug hunt, bug hunt" under his breath as he went back to work on the shapes.

They were all quiet for a few minutes.

Gwilym spoke first. "Life seems almost normal sometimes. I can't believe how blue the sky is here."

"It's like that, especially in the winter. Interested in another craft beer?" Logan asked.

"Always," Gwilym grinned.

"I'll be back in a minute."

When Logan returned with two cold beers, Charlie wasn't there.

"Where's Charlie?" Logan asked.

"He wanted to show Zoey and Nina his shapes. He turned a couple of them into bugs with faces and wings." Gwilym laughed. "He's a creative little bugger. He said he'd be back in a minute." He took a sip of the beer. "Excellent. I'm going to miss this when I go home."

"When are you planning on leaving?"

"I want to make sure Nina is safe first." Gwilym looked at Logan. "Just between you and me, I'm going to ask her to go with me. She can stay in Vancouver for a few days or the rest of her life. I'll leave it up to her. Do you think she'll want to go with me?"

Logan smiled. "Nina likes you a lot. I've never seen her take to a dude so quickly. And I'll add that you're a much better option for her than her last boyfriend. So yes, it's definitely worth asking her. I want to see her happy."

Just then, another car rolled up to the curb in front of Casa Pacifica and stopped. A tall man exited the car. He had a reddish-brown complexion, dark eyes, aquiline features, and black hair almost touching his collar. He approached them.

"Hello, my name is Cass Cosay. I'd like to speak to your manager."

"I'm the manager. My name is Logan Reid. How can I help you?" He gestured to a seat at the table, and Cass Cosay sat down.

"I heard you have an apartment that will be available soon. I'm interested in renting."

Logan shook his head. "Sorry. I've rented it already. The new tenant has already signed the lease. She'll be moving in soon."

Suddenly, Charlie came running out of the main front door of the building. "Daddy!" Daddy!" His voice was strained, and he was very close to tears. He stood about three feet away from Logan, his face red, his right arm and hand pointing up toward Nina's apartment on the second floor. He was trembling all over.

"What's wrong?" Logan was very alarmed. His cheerful little boy was clearly terrified.

"This bad man has Nina all tied up and he wanted to tie me up and Zoey said she would trade herself for me and the bad man laughed and said I could go but he had to see Zoey's tits. She told me to run fast and find you, and then he hit Zoey. I don't know what 'tits' means."

By this time, all three men were already on their feet. Logan grabbed Charlie and took off running. He was first up the front stairs, with Gwilym and the man called Cass right behind him. Logan stopped at his front door, and the other two started up the stairs. Cass reached out and touched Gwilym's arm. He put a finger to his lips indicating that they should be quiet.

Logan opened his front door and sat Charlie down inside his apartment. "Charlie, I'm going to close and lock the door. Do not let anyone in. Understand? Stay here and don't let anyone in."

Charlie nodded. His eyes were full of tears.

"You can watch cartoons. I'll get you some ice cream when I come back. Stay inside and don't open the door. Promise?"

"I promise." Tears started rolling down his cheeks.

Logan closed the door and locked it. He followed Gwilym and Cass up the stairs. They stopped at the top of the stairs, just outside Nina's door.

"You don't have to get involved," Logan whispered. "The guy is a wanna-be killer."

Cass Cosay pulled a thin black leather folder out of his pocket and flipped it open. He held it up. Logan and Gwilym both could see big letters that said "FBI" and "Special Agent" in smaller letters. Above that were the words, "Department of Justice." A photo of Cass with his name took up a section on the right side of the identification card.

Logan's eyebrows went up in surprise. Gwilym gasped.

Cass slowly and carefully cracked the door open. That meant Cass, Gwilym and Logan could hear what was going on inside.

"Do you bitches hear something?" the man inside growled.

"Charlie is watching cartoons," Nina managed to speak. "I can hear the cartoons."

The man laughed, an odd strangled sort of laughter that sounded close to hysteria.

"Okay, let's get down to business. Nina, know what I'm going to do to you?"

There were a few seconds of silence.

"No? I'm going to tie your hands to this table. Then I'm going to smash every bone in your fingers. Every single fucking bone. You will never ever be able to play the piano again. Your life as a jazz pianist is over, you bitch."

Logan looked at Gwilym. His face was a dark red, and Logan could see a muscle in his jaw flexing. Gwilym looked like he would like nothing better than to smash the door down and tear Ethan Reddick into bloody little pieces.

"And you, Miss Blonde Pony Tail. Since I have you tied up now, maybe I'll have a go at you first. I'm gonna want more than just a look. I'd say you need some dick." He laughed again. "You can watch, Nina."

Logan was shaking his head no. This worthless piece of shit was threatening to rape Zoey. No way. No way. No way. Logan was *not* going to let that piece of shit so much as touch Zoey Corban. No way.

Cass reached out and again touched his finger to his lips. He shook his head no, a warning to stay quiet. He turned toward the door and closed it silently. He knocked loudly on the door.

Another moment of silence. Then Nina spoke in a strangled voice. "Who's there?"

"I have your order ready, Miss…"

"Perry," Logan whispered.

"Yeah, Miss Perry. I have your order from the taco stand. They put some guacamole in, too. You wanted a side-order of guacamole. Right?"

There was just a moment of silence.

Then Ethan Reddick spoke loudly. "Leave it outside the door."

"I have to get paid for the order," Cass said.

"Okay. Okay. Okay."

Cass motioned for Logan and Gwilym to stand close to the wall so Reddick couldn't see them.

Ethan Reddick opened the door, the gun in his hand pointed at Cass. "Leave the food and get lost."

That's all it took. Cass reached out and grabbed the hand that held the gun. He pushed Reddick's arm and hand upward, then shoved the man. Reddick stumbled backward. The gun went off, and a bullet struck the wall just above Nina's door.

Cass pushed Reddick further back into Nina's apartment. He twisted the gun out of Reddick's hand in a quick move, then kicked the back of Reddick's knees. Reddick fell hard to the floor onto his knees. Cass turned his body and twisted his arms behind him. A plastic tie appeared from Cass's back pocket. He closed it around Reddick's wrists and tightened it, immobilizing him.

Reddick squealed in protest.

"Be quiet." Cass pulled his identification card out again and flashed it in front of Reddick's face. "FBI. You're under arrest."

Gwilym went directly to Nina, and Logan went directly to Zoey.

"Are you okay?" Gwilym asked. "Did he hit you?"

Nina was struggling to speak. "I'm not hurt. He was going to crush my fingers. He was going to ruin me. I wouldn't be able to play piano ever again." Her eyes filled with tears.

Gwilym had untied her and pulled her to her feet. His arms were around her now, holding her.

Logan crouched down next to Zoey. He reached out and touched her cheek. "Oh my god, Zoey. He hit you. There's blood on your face. Your lips. Your eye is all bruised." He looked down and saw that Reddick had torn open her blouse. He could see that her bra was visible. He pulled the blouse closer to cover her. "That piece of shit. I want to…" He gritted his teeth.

"I'm okay. I'm okay, Logan. I've been hurt worse in soccer games. I'll survive." Zoey began to giggle. "What an asshole!"

"I'm going to take care of you, Zoey. Let's go down to my apartment. I'll clean up all this blood. I have to call the cops first."

"Okay. Yes. Cops first." Zoey smiled. "Thank you, Logan."

Logan stood and pulled his phone out of his pocket. He turned to Cass. "I'm calling the police officer I spoke with, Officer Alvarez."

Cass nodded. "I already called 9-1-1. Glad to hear you have someone already working on this case."

Reddick started to complain. His hands and arms hurt. His knees hurt. He had been mistreated. He claimed police brutality.

Cass knelt down beside him and said in a low voice, "You know what my people used to do to white guys like you?"

Reddick's eyes got big.

"We Apache drank the white man's blood. I think you should shut up now."

Reddick stopped talking.

The sound of sirens came closer and stopped in front of the apartment building. Two cops jumped out of the first patrol car and mounted the stairs, guns drawn. They burst into Nina's apartment, and found Cass standing there, both hands in the air, one hand holding his FBI identification. Gwilym was still holding Nina. Logan stood, looked at Cass, and put his hands in the air, too.

Officer Alvarez followed the two policemen into the apartment. He nodded at Logan who put his hands down. Cass had already done the same.

Alvarez looked closely at Cass's FBI identification then said to Cass, "Welcome to Tucson, Mr. Cosay."

"Thank you. Once you get this guy hauled off, we can touch base," Cass said to Alvarez.

Cass pulled Reddick to his feet. Reddick said nothing, his eyes darting back and forth between Alvarez and Cass. Cass removed the plastic tie and one of the cops replaced it with handcuffs.

Alvarez spoke directly to Reddick. "We're arresting you for two cases of attempted murder, taking and holding hostages, and bodily injury to a hostage." He glanced at Zoey. "Now I'm going to read you your Miranda rights, Mr. Reddick," Alvarez continued. "You have the right to remain silent. Anything you say or do can and will be held against you in a court of law. You have the right to speak to an attorney. If you cannot afford an attorney, one will be appointed for you. Do you understand these rights as they have been read to you?"

"Yes," Reddick whispered.

"Take him in," Alvarez said to the two cops. "I'll follow right behind you."

"Where are you taking him?" Logan asked.

"To the Pima County Detention Center. He'll be enjoying the hospitality of the Pima County Sheriff's Department for an undetermined period of time."

Logan nodded. "What a relief. We're all safe now."

"I believe so," Alvarez said. "We had a good lead on Reddick from a couple of security cameras, but it looks like Reddick found you before we found him."

"Thank you for coming so quickly," Logan said. He turned to Cass. "And thank you for all you did. You've been invaluable."

Cass nodded. "Just doing my job." He reached into his wallet and handed a card to Logan. "You can reach me here. If you have an opening in your building, please let me know. And it would be best if you do not mention to anyone that I am an FBI agent." He looked at Gwilym as well as Logan. Both men nodded.

Officer Alvarez and Cass Cosay both said goodbye and left at the same time.

Logan and Gwilym turned to Zoey and Nina who were huddled in a corner holding each others' hands and whispering to each other.

"Zoey," Logan said, "let's go downstairs to my place, and I'll try to get some of that blood off of you. Charlie will be glad to see us both. He was really scared."

"Take Charlie's homework with you," Nina said. "Tell him I like the circle with the wings best of all."

Logan gathered Charlie's papers and said goodbye. He took Zoey's hand, and they headed downstairs.

Gwilym pulled Nina to her feet and put his arms around her. After a while, he pulled back and looked her in the eyes.

"My darling girl. We need to have a talk."

Nina smiled. "No, not yet, my darling boy. First, we're going to follow the jazz lines."

Gwilym laughed as she led him to her bedroom.

10 Changes

Logan woke early as usual. He was not rested because he'd had several bad dreams in the night. Dreams about Charlie getting hurt. Dreams about Zoey getting hurt. Dreams that he couldn't do anything to prevent this. Dreams that someone he loved would die. Nightmares, really.

"Let it go, let it go," he muttered to himself. "It's only dreams. Just dreams."

His thoughts turned again to yesterday afternoon when he and Zoey went to his apartment after the police left. As he'd unlocked his door, he called out, "Charlie!"

Charlie came running. He threw himself at Logan. "Daddy!" Logan held him and hugged him tightly. Charlie looked at Zoey. "Zoey, you're bleeding!"

"Not to worry," Zoey grinned. "That bad guy hit me. But I told your dad that I've been hurt worse in soccer games so I'll be fine."

"Give me a minute, and I'll get our first aid kit and see if I can get this blood cleaned up. You may have to have stitches or something. Charlie, see if Zoey needs a drink."

Charlie took Zoey's hand. "Want some juice? Or milk?"

"I'd like some water, actually. Do you have any water?"

"I'll get you some. I don't like that bad guy."

"Don't worry. The police took him to jail. We're all safe now."

"He went to jail?"

"Yes, we're safe now."

"I'll get you some water." Charlie ran to the kitchen.

Logan returned with the first aid kit and one of his cotton, long-sleeve shirts.

"He tore your blouse. Want to wear this? It's one of my mine. It will be too big for you, but at least you can button it up."

Zoey slipped her blouse off. Logan's eyes widened. He turned and looked in the other direction.

When he turned to look at Zoey again, she was rolling up the sleeves of his shirt. "Yes, it's too big, but at least my bra isn't showing. I'll return it to you later after I've washed it."

Charlie returned with a glass of cold water, and Zoey took a long drink. Then Logan started the process of carefully removing the dried blood from Zoey's face with gauze and cotton and a little water. "Looks like you're going to have a black eye. Your lip is busted. I'll put some hydrogen peroxide on the cuts to stop infection, but I don't think you need any stitches."

Zoey nodded. "Thank you, Logan."

Logan sat back and took both of Zoey's hands in his. "No, I'm the one who must thank you. You traded yourself for my son. You rescued Charlie from a very bad situation, and you kept him safe. I have no words to express the depth of my gratitude."

Charlie came and put his arms around Zoey's shoulders. "Thank you, Zoey."

"Oh, you two. You're too much." She shook her head and smiled.

"We owe you," Logan said.

Zoey's face changed. She giggled. "Okay. I'll remember that."

Logan and Charlie nodded seriously.

Zoey stood up. "Thanks for the first aid. I need to go home now and continue packing."

"Do you need a ride?" Logan asked.

"No. My car is in the faculty parking lot at Tucson High. It's just a short walk."

Logan turned to Charlie. "How about if we escort Zoey to her car?"

"Okay," the little boy said. "What does 'escort' mean?"

"Just go walk with her to her car."

Charlie looked up at Zoey. "Daddy and I are going to escort you."

"Excellent. May I hold your hand as we walk?"

"Of course," Charlie said in a serious tone of voice.

On their walk to the parking lot, Logan said, "If you move into your new apartment this weekend, I could help. Do you need some help? I'd be happy to do whatever."

"I'll be moving in on Sunday because I have a game I'm coaching on Saturday. I hired two big, strong senior boys from my biology class to help me haul my stuff. They are both football players. Big boys. It won't take long for me to move in."

Now it was the next morning, and Logan actually felt better remembering this interaction with Zoey and Charlie. He stretched and yawned again. Yes, everything was back to normal. Get up. Shower. Make coffee. Wake up Charlie. Get him some breakfast and walk him to school.

Yes, everything was back to normal. Or so it seemed. But was it normal for him to be thinking about Zoey so much?

~~~

Nina and Gwilym woke up in a state of bliss, wrapped in each others' arms.

"I'm getting up now," he whispered.

"Oh, no. Please don't go." She snuggled closer.

"I need some coffee, and so do you."

Nina groaned. "I'll miss you."

Gwilym was on his feet, dressed, and in the kitchen making coffee five minutes later. As the coffee brewed, he could hear Nina in the shower. She joined him a little while later.

"You are very beautiful," Gwilym told her. To him, she appeared to be glowing.

"If I'm beautiful, it's because I feel so good," she grinned. "That's all your fault. You made me feel really, really good." She began singing in a low voice Nina Simone's classic, "Feeling Good."

Gwilym watched her as she sang. When she finished the song, he said, "Beautiful. Sit down and I'll pour you a cuppa."

They sat together at Nina's dining table, quiet, content, holding hands.

Gwilym looked away, then back to Nina. "Sorry to disturb this happiness with you, but I have to talk with you about something."

"You're going to tell me you have to leave." Her smile had disappeared. "I don't want you to go."

"I have to go. I have responsibilities at home. But I have an idea, a proposal really. I think you should go with me to Vancouver." There. He'd said it. He had no idea how she would react. Gwilym decided to make an argument. "You can go for a couple of weeks. Or you can stay for a long time. Or forever. If you stay, we can come back to Tucson frequently. Whenever you want. For as long as you want. Whatever makes you happy. As for me, that's what I want. I want to make you happy. I want you to be safe and happy and focus on your music. So think about it. Think about going with me. Please."

Nina looked out the window to the south. The sky was that intense blue that was so characteristic of the Sonoran Desert in winter.

She turned and looked at Gwilym. "Okay."

"Okay?"

"Okay." She smiled.

"You'll go with me?"

"Yes. When do we leave?"

Gwilym laughed. "Okay!" Joy. Overwhelming joy. "We'll leave in a few days. We have to make arrangements first. Say goodbye to your bookstore job, goodbye to your friends and family, and pack up a few things. I'll make a deal with Logan to keep this apartment for you, maybe sublet it. Then we can stay here when we come back for the jazz fest and other trips back."

"Sounds good." She leaned forward and kissed him. "Logan will like that."

"This was too easy," Gwilym said. "I was afraid you'd say no."

Nina laughed. "And lose you? No way." She took another sip of coffee. "I guess I'd better start packing."

"And I'll get us plane tickets."

"Or we could go back to bed." Nina smiled.

"Or we could go back to bed." Gwilym nodded. He had never been so happy.

~~~

Sunday afternoon. Charlie was up and running around in circles in the living room, pretending to be a bird again. No. Not a bird. Charlie made it clear that this time, he was a bat. Logan dodged him, trying to tidy up a bit because the apartment would be full of people in a few hours for the weekly Sunday potluck.

Everyone would be there except Marc who still hadn't called Logan to say when he was returning with that big dog.

So that meant Nina and Gwilym, Frida, Li, Dylan, and Zoey, as well as Logan and Charlie, would all be here soon. And Logan had invited Cass Cosay who had arranged to sublet Nina's apartment for an undetermined length of time. Cass hadn't given Logan a lot of information, but Logan got the distinct impression that Cass was on a job, and for reasons unknown to Logan, Cass would be using Nina's apartment for surveillance purposes. Maybe. Logan didn't really know much about how FBI agents operated.

"Charlie, did you like that yogurt smoothie I made you for breakfast?"

"Hell, yeah!"

Logan rolled his eyes. "Don't talk like that."

Charlie giggled. "Yes, sir, Daddy sir. I loved that yogurt smoothie."

"I suggest you ask Zoey this evening if she has more good ideas for breakfast, not those nasty cereal ring thingies."

"Will do, sir, Daddy sir." More giggles.

What a smart ass. This child is going to be a handful when he's a teenager, Logan muttered to himself. Maybe he could get some help from Zoey on how to handle Charlie. He stopped and shook his head. Thinking about Zoey again. Zoey ten years from now when Charlie is a teenager? What the hell? Don't get ahead of yourself, Logan Reid.

The afternoon came and went, and soon residents in the apartment building began to drift in for the evening potluck, each carrying at least one container full of food. Gwilym brought more wine and ice cream. They gathered around the table, each with a glass of wine, except for Charlie who drank fruit juice. Cass Cosay was the last one to arrive. He brought with him something he called Apache cheese bread. It was a baked bread with some unexpected ingredients like chopped ham, green peppers, and onions. And cheese, too. The Apache bread was very popular. Everyone complimented Cass, and Charlie ate two pieces of the bread.

At one point, Cass and Logan were alone in the kitchen.

"I heard what you said to Reddick about drinking the white man's blood." Logan grinned. "I take it you're Apache?"

Cass nodded. "White Mountain tribe."

"I think you scared the bejesus out of him." Logan chuckled.

Cass smiled. "That was the idea. Fact is, though, we Apache don't really like white man's blood. Not very tasty."

"You're going to fit in well here," Logan grinned.

Before they began eating, Logan stood and raised his wine glass. "Thanks to all of you for coming. Li, it's good to see you back home." Li nodded and waved. Li's arm was in a sling, but he'd managed to bring a Chinese noodle soup with some help from Frida who carried the pot. Logan and everyone took a sip of wine.

"I'd like to say goodbye, for a while anyway, to Nina who is going to live in Vancouver with Gwilym. I know she'll be back, and Gwilym will come with her. So we'll see them both again."

"*Buen viaje!*" "Have a good trip." Another sip of wine for all.

"And I'd like to introduce Cass Cosay who will be subletting Nina's apartment," Logan continued.

"What do you do?" Li asked. "Spend all your time making great breads?"

Cass grinned. "Actually I am very interested in cooking and baking. I've started researching a book about food ways of the American Southwest Native American tribes. I'll be focusing on Apache, Navajo, Comanche, and Tohono O'odham."

"Yay!" Charlie called out. "That's a great idea. I like food."

Everyone laughed.

"Actually," Dylan looked directly at Cass, "it is an excellent idea. I look forward to seeing the book when it's finished. Maybe you could try your recipes out on us."

Everyone agreed.

Logan was surprised. Was this true or did Cass make all this up to distract from his FBI investigative work? Who knew?

"Finally, I'd like to introduce Zoey Corban who has moved into the apartment downstairs. She is a welcome relief to Tick and Bugger who were in that apartment for way too long."

Zoey grinned and waved. "I'm a biology teacher at Tucson High." Everyone extended their welcome.

"Zoey likes bugs," Charlie said.

"Edible bugs?" Cass asked.

"What's that mean?" Charlie looked confused.

"Bugs you can eat."

"Oh, yuck. Zoey, can you eat bugs?"

Zoey looked at Cass and shook her head no, laughing. "Charlie, yes, you can eat some bugs but other bugs will make you really sick. So don't eat a bug unless you ask me first."

"Okay." Charlie looked at Cass. "Do you eat bugs?"

"Not really. I prefer cheese bread."

Charlie looked relieved.

The pot luck dinner was amiable as usual. Food, good conversation, and more wine followed. The hour came for Charlie to go to bed. While Logan was with him, everyone cleaned up the dishes. When Logan returned, they sat for a while and chatted with each other. The evening began to wind down, and time came for everyone to go.

Zoey was last to leave Logan's apartment. "Thank you, Logan. This was a lovely potluck. I had a lot of fun."

"We do this every week. I hope you'll come every Sunday evening."

She looked up at him. "I'll just give you a quick hug." She did just that. Then she was gone.

Logan watched her walk down the hall to the door of her new apartment. She unlocked the door, turned and waved at him, and she went inside, locking the door behind her. Logan felt a sudden wave of contentment wash over him. He closed the door and went to check on Charlie.

Thank you from the Author:

Hello Reader!

Thank you for reading *Take Four*, the first Iron Horse Mystery. Please leave a review of this book wherever you buy books (Amazon, Kobo, Nook, Apple, etc.) and also at Bookbub and Goodreads. By leaving a review for others to read, you can make it much easier for mystery readers everywhere to find this book. Thank you so much. Please sign up for my monthly newsletter all about art, books, and the natural world at www.cjshane.com/contactnewsletter.html

If you are curious about the jazz music in this book, here are some links:

Nina Simone: "Feelin' Good" https://www.youtube.com/watch?v=oHs98TEYecM

Dave Brubeck Quartet: "Take Five" https://www.youtube.com/watch?v=PHdU5sHigYQ

Iron Horse Neighborhood

The term "iron horse" refers both to steam-powered locomotives and also to the iron rails upon which the iron
horse traveled. The term dates back to as early as 1825 with
the first locomotives, and it became common both in the
U.S. and in the United Kingdom.

The iron horse came to Tucson for the first time in the
1880s with the arrival of Southern Pacific Railroad. Hundreds of railroad employees arrived as well to create the
railroad that would lead eventually to southern California. Tucson became the location for rail repairs as well.

Southern Pacific required its employees to live within a
mile of the railroad so the workers could hear the whistle
that called them to work and to alert them to emergen-
cies. The Iron Horse neighborhood was just north of the
east-west railroad and within hearing distance of the work
whistle. So that's how the neighborhood was born and became located just north of modern Broadway Boulevard.

Workers' jobs included train engineers, firemen, brake-
men, and conductors as well as laborers who did the hard
work of building the tracks. The rail workers represented
Irish, German, Scottish and Polish ancestry. Some 85%
were blue collar workers, and 15% worked as clerks or in
other positions for Southern Pacific. Wives and children

came with some the male workers, too. As early as 1883, residents petitioned the local school district to open a school in the Iron Horse neighborhood. But funds were lacking for repairing the local building chosen for the school or to hire a teacher. Consequently, the Iron Horse neighborhood school didn't open until 1899. The building designated for the first Iron Horse school still exists.

Because of the many employment opportunities, hundreds of men migrated to Tucson to work for the railroad. They lived in bungalows and small single family homes, apartments, duplexes and row houses. Over the years and into the twentieth century, the architecture of the neighborhood varied, and included Queen Anne, Sonoran adobe, Territorial, and Craftsman styles.

Workers were not the only ones to flock to Tucson. The railroad also brought in tourists, probably because of the warm, sunny winters, and also many were heading west to California. Tucsonans still welcome tourists who migrate here for winter. Locals call them "snowbirds."

The Iron Horse neighborhood residents today still includes family homeowners and apartment renters, including students from the nearby University of Arizona, northeast of Iron Horse. Downtown Tucson is just to the south and west of Iron Horse. The neighborhood is noted for its architecture, its walking and biking paths, and for small businesses, too, such as the New Empire Food Market on 9th Street, which has served the neighborhood since the 1930s.

Iron Horse neighborhood became a part of the National Registry of Historic Places in 1889. Residents can still hear the passing trains, now known as Union Pacific, which blow their horns regularly as they pass by.

IRON HORSE NEXT IN SERIES?
SHADOW MAN

1 Sunday Potluck

Logan Reid stuck tiny candles into several little plastic candle holders, then he carefully placed the candles into the soft surface of the birthday cake resting on his dining room table. He had no idea how old Frida was, but it was her birthday, she was a part of the Casa Pacifica family, and he was determined to provide her and the others with a birthday cake. He'd bought the cake at a nearby bakery earlier that afternoon. When he returned home, he decided to decorate the cake with twelve candles, one for each month. He was pretty sure Frida would like that. Maybe. He guessed maybe she'd like it. He hoped, anyway.

The problem was that Logan had no idea what he was doing. When he was growing up, those birthday cakes always seemed to appear magically, thanks to his mother. And in the years that he was married, his wife Caroline took care of this kind of stuff. But Caroline was gone now, with nothing left but the memory of their lives together and her sudden death. Three and a half years ago.

Logan shook his head. "Stop brooding," he muttered to himself. Life was good, wasn't it? He was manager of the Casa Pacifica Apartments, so his rent was low. He and the tenants had formed a peculiar little family. They helped each other out, and they ate pot luck dinners with each other every Sunday evening. He had his grad-student teaching job at the university, and he was about to get his PhD in May. Best of all, his five-year-old son, Charlie, was healthy and seemed happy most of the time. Logan's life revolved around Charlie.

Suddenly, an image of one of the Casa Pacifica tenants slipped into his consciousness. Zoey Corban. She was sweet and pretty and fun to be around, and she clearly adored Charlie. Logan trusted her, and because of that, he allowed Charlie to go do things with her when Logan wasn't present. After Zoey had traded herself for Charlie so he could escape a crazed killer, Logan trusted her completely with his precious son. Not many people would put themselves under a killer's control so that someone else's child could go free. Logan hoped that Zoey would come to the pot luck and help them all celebrate Frida's birthday.

The door to his apartment flew open, and Charlie ran into the room. Zoey was close behind.

"Daddy, we found some!"

Logan looked up and was pleased to see Zoey grinning at him. He returned her smile. Earlier in the afternoon, she'd come by and asked Charlie if he wanted to go on a "bug hunt." Charlie's enthusiastic response was to jump up and down and squeal, "Yes! A bug hunt! A bug hunt!" They had been gone almost three hours.

"What did you find?" Logan asked.

"Some dragonflies. We took pictures. Zoey said we could collect the dragonflies, but she thinks it's better to just let them live their lives. So Zoey took photos. She's going to share the photos with me. I'm going to make a bug scrapbook."

"So you went to the river?"

"Yes," Zoey said. "Charlie, which river did we visit?"

"The Santa Cruz!" Charlie was dancing around in a circle now. "We saw some Pond Damsel dragonflies that are called American Bluets."

"You're teaching him the correct names?" Logan smiled again at Zoey.

"Definitely. The word 'bug' just won't cut it." Zoey laughed. "I'm a biology teacher at the high school, remember?"

Suddenly Charlie noticed the birthday cake. He approached and stared at it. Then he turned to Logan and asked, "Can I have some cake?"

Logan nodded. "Yes, but this is Frida's birthday cake so we'll have it for dessert this evening. We'll sing 'Happy Birthday,' and she has to blow out the candles first." He looked at Zoey. "I hope you'll come to the potluck this evening."

"I wouldn't miss it for the world." She turned toward the door. "I need to go home and make something to bring to the pot luck."

Charlie ran to her and gave her a big hug. "Thank you for taking me on a bug hunt."

"Thank you for going with me." Zoe grinned. She smoothed down his wayward, tousled blond hair. "We'll do it again sometime."

Charlie started his spins around the room again, singing "Bug hunt! Bug hunt!"

She waved goodbye, and Logan returned the wave. "Thanks, Zoey."

She nodded and closed the door behind her.

"Charlie, bath time."

"Do I have to?"

Logan was always amazed at how Charlie's happy tone could instantly turn into whining when a bath was mentioned. And it was odd how he seemed to enjoy himself once he got into the bath water. Getting there was the problem.

"Yes, you have to take a bath. I can see dried mud on your legs. And hurry up. Everyone will arrive soon."

"Okay. Okay." Charlie sighed and headed toward the bathroom.

"And put those muddy shoes outside the bathroom door. I'll clean them up later."

"Zoey said I need some wading boots."

"Okay. We'll talk about that later. Focus on the bath."

Logan waited until he could hear the bathwater running, then he went to the kitchen to check on a pan of lasagna in the oven. He surprised himself. He was actually starting to like cooking. Sometimes. He heard a soft knock on the door.

"Logan, it's me."

Logan recognized the voice of Cass Cosay who was staying in the apartment on the second floor just above Logan and Charlie's ground floor apartment.

"Come on in."

Cass opened the door and entered. He was carrying a plate of muffins. "I bought some mesquite meal at the San Javier Co-op Farm, and I added it to the muffin recipe. They turned out pretty good. The mesquite gives the muffins a nice, nutty flavor." Cass Cosay was a tall, muscular man, with a reddish-brown complexion that revealed his Apache Native American heritage. His black hair had grown out some, and he wore it in a knot at the back of his head.

Logan took the plate and placed it on the table. "San Javier? That's the Tohono O'odham farm. Thanks for making these muffins. I'm glad you're here because I've been wanting to talk to you about how things are going. I haven't seen much of you lately."

During the altercation with the would-be killer that held Casa Pacifica residents Nina Perry and Zoey Corban as hostages, Cass had revealed to Logan and Canadian visitor Gwilym Havard that he was an FBI agent. Cass took down the villain, disarmed and arrested him, and freed both Zoey and Nina.

"Everything is going well," Cass said. "My team and I were able to identify a group of smugglers and drug dealers working out of Fourth Avenue, quite near here. We made several arrests."

"Smuggling what? Drugs?"

"They were smuggling the chemicals used to make fentanyl pills. The chemicals are imported into Mexico from China. Usually the fentanyl pills are made in Sonora in northern Mexico, then smuggled across the border into the U.S. We're trying to figure out why they've started smuggling the chemicals across the border. We're thinking that they have been manufacturing the drug here as well as in Mexico. We caught them selling the pills, too, and now we're looking for where exactly they made the drug. The fact that they were selling the chemicals here also suggests that there might be other gangs who have entered the market and are making the drug here as well."

"That drug, fentanyl, I mean, scares me to death," Logan said. "It looks like candy."

"Yes. Very dangerous. Kids and teens sometimes think they are eating candy. Death comes really fast."

"I'm glad you arrested a bunch of them. How's it working out for you to live here?"

"Good. This Iron Horse neighborhood is pretty quiet, but it's close enough to all the action so I don't have to go very far to get involved. I like the apartment here, too. It's comfortable, and you and the other tenants are good people. I'm actually thinking about taking a little break from work for a while since we made these arrests. If it's okay, I'd like to continue staying here."

"No problem. Gwilym paid the rent in advance. After what you did, rescuing Nina and Zoey from that nutcase with the gun, you can stay as long as Nina and Gwilym agree. I can't predict really what will happen with them. Nina loves Vancouver, and she loves Gwilym even more. They might come back to Tucson just for visits but live most of the time in B.C." Logan looked into the oven again. "Ten more minutes, I'd say."

"That smells great."

"I also wanted to ask you. Are you keeping it a secret that you're an FBI agent? Earlier, you told Gwilym and me not to mention that to anyone."

"I used to work undercover most of the time so I definitely didn't want anyone to know then that I'm FBI. My job changed over time, and now I'm a Special Agent with other duties. I'm not undercover, and don't plan to be, so my job isn't really a secret now. However, I don't usually advertise what I do. In fact, I stay pretty quiet about it. But, sometimes, I do tell people if they seem okay."

"I think all of us feel safer with you here."

Suddenly a loud voice came from the bathroom. "Daddy! There's something in the water!"

Logan headed for the bathroom. He came back in a few minutes, shaking his head. "Another bug. He's saving it to show to Zoey."

Cass chuckled. "Ah, the important things in life. Bugs in the bathtub."

A series of knocks on Logan's door was followed by the entrance of the other friends, also tenants, in the apartment building. The seven Casa Pacifica apartments were located in what had been a railroad executive's home, built in 1920s in the Spanish Revival style. Later, the apartments were created from the original home. The apartments were spacious, and all had large windows that looked out on the mesquite trees in the side yard and the tree-lined street in the front.

Li arrived next. His real name was Liang, thanks to his Chinese heritage, but Li was easier. He worked as a chef at a leading Chinese restaurant. Zoey, the biology teacher and bug hunter, came next. Then Frida, the birthday girl, arrived. Frida was a bartender who spent most of her free time organizing labor protests. Last to arrive was Dylan, the accountant. The only tenant still missing was Marc, a photojournalist who was on assignment and not currently in Tucson. Each one placed their dishes on the large dining table.

Logan had his lasagna out of the oven now and on a trivet on the table. "I'll set the table. My helper who usually sets the table isn't being very helpful. He's still in the bath." Logan went to fetch plates and silverware. But, first, he turned to Zoey. "Could you go see about Charlie? It's time to eat, and he's still playing around in the bathwater. He has a bug to show you."

Zoey nodded, grinning. "He's going to be an excellent entomologist." She headed for the bathroom.

"What the hell is an entomologist?" Frida grinned.

"Someone who studies bugs," Logan replied.

"Oh, how exciting." Frida made a face.

Cass found himself taking a long look at Dylan. He was very curious about her. Okay, yeah. She's a looker, he said to himself. Her long, auburn hair was lovely, and she was very pretty. She was quiet, and didn't rattle on like some of the others. He liked that about her, too. But mostly, he wondered how someone could go from being a professional tattoo artist to a certified public accountant. He wanted to know more about her.

Zoey managed to get Charlie out of the bath, dried off, dressed, and at the table in record time. When they joined everyone, Zoey said to Logan in a low voice, "Pinacate beetle. That's what Charlie found. A pinacate beetle."

Logan chuckled. "Good to know." He poured wine for everyone, and juice for Charlie.

Li stood and said, "I'm making the toast tonight. To Frida!" He raised his wineglass. "What we all love about Frida is her energy, her optimism, and her persistence. All those corporate types who resist unionization and better working conditions for their employees better watch out and stay on Frida's good side, or they will be sorry!"

"Hear. Hear. To Frida!" were the words heard around the table.

"Want to say anything, Frida?" Logan asked.

Frida stood and grinned at everyone. "Thank you for this potluck. Thank you for your love and support. You are the best family I've ever had." She turned to Li. "And thank you, Li, for finding my kitty Bonita when she got out the other day. A coyote could have eaten her in one big bite. So thank you so much!"

"Can I play with Bonita again?" Charlie asked.

"Of course. Maybe you could stay with me for a while and play with Bonita when your daddy goes on a date." Frida looked at Logan and grinned, then noticeably shifted her gaze to Zoey. Logan turned pink, and Zoey looked down at her hands. Those two had a reputation among the Casa Pacifica friends for being in the early stages of a romance, but both seemed too shy to move forward. Frida was doing her best to help them get over themselves and take the next step.

"So let's eat!" Frida declared.

After stuffing themselves and, at the same time, chatting constantly, Logan began to collect the dishes. Dylan and Zoey helped him to move everything back into the kitchen. Zoey handed small plates to Charlie, and he distributed them to every place at the table.

Logan brought the cake out and lit the candles. "Make a wish, Frida, and blow out your candles."

Frida pressed her hand against her heart and closed her eyes. When she opened them again, she bent forward and blew out all the candles. Everyone cheered and sang "Happy Birthday" to her.

Li laughed. "You can bet Frida's wish has to do with that new contract she's negotiating with the grocery store chain."

Frida grinned. "I'm not saying anything. I want my wish to come true."

After an hour of amiable conversation, Charlie said goodnight, and, with Logan's help, he went to bed. When Logan returned, Cass stood and smiled at everyone. "Happy Birthday, Frida. It's time for me to say goodnight. I just finished a job, and I'm taking a little time off so I'll see you around."

After he'd closed the door behind him, Li and Frida both asked Logan at the same time, "What's his job?"

Logan hesitated. "Cass is in law enforcement. If you want details, you can ask him. The job he just finished had to do with taking down some drug dealers."

Everyone nodded approvingly.

"I'm next," Dylan said. She stood and waved to Frida. "Happy Birthday, girlfriend. And many more."

Frida whispered to Dylan before she could get away. "Are you going to go check out Cass?"

"Yep. And I'm not shy."

"I know you're not. I like the idea of another romance developing in Casa Pacifica. Cass is a hottie." Frida grinned.

"I'm just curious about him. That's all." Dylan smiled. "I'm going to fetch a sweater. It's chilly this evening. Happy Birthday again, Frida."

Sunset had come already, and the evening sky was dusky. Dylan found Cass sitting out in the side yard. She approached him.

"Okay to sit with you for a little while?" Dylan asked. "This is my favorite time of day."

He turned toward her and smiled. "Sure. Have a seat."

They sat in easy silence for a few minutes.

Cass turned toward her and said, "You want to know something, don't you?"

Dylan chuckled. "Yes, I do. I'd like to get to know you a little better."

"Good. Same here. I'd like to know you better." Cass was both curious and pleased.

More silence. Finally Dylan said, "Okay, I'll start. I'm an animal lover."

"I am, too."

"My favorites are horses and dogs."

He turned toward her, surprised. "Me, too. Dogs I get, but why horses?"

"I grew up on a horse farm in Kentucky. I've always lived around horses. They are lovely creatures. So full of heart. So loving."

Cass nodded. "I grew up on a horse farm like you."

"You did?" Dylan was genuinely surprised.

"Yes, I grew up near a little town called Whiteriver on the Fort Apache Reservation north of here. My people are Western Apache, White Mountain tribe."

"So you know all about horses?"

Cass nodded. "I do. I'd rather spend time with a horse than with most people."

"I can agree with that," Dylan said. "I have a horse now. I board her at a stable on the far east side of Tucson, and

I go out on the weekends for rides. She's an old girl now so we go easy on the rides. Her name is Betty."

"Betty?" Cass chuckled.

"I was a kid when she and I bonded. I thought that name was perfect for her back then. When I moved out here, she came with me."

"That must have been a big deal, bringing a horse with you all the way from Kentucky."

Dylan shrugged her shoulders. "She's been a lot of trouble and a big expense. But she's my best friend, and I want to make sure she has a good life until the end."

More quiet.

"Okay. So you know all about me. Tell me something about you." Dylan looked at him.

"Well, I don't really know *all* about you. I'd like to know more. But I get what you're saying. So what would you like to know about me?" Cass smiled.

"When you left the potluck, Frida and Li asked Logan what kind of work you do. He said law enforcement, and we're supposed to ask you if we want to know more."

"Sure you want to know?"

Dylan nodded. "I want to know."

"I'm an FBI Special Agent."

"Interesting. So how did you get from a kid on a horse farm on the reservation to being an FBI Special Agent."

Cass shook his head and chuckled. "I don't usually talk about this, but I guess I'll tell you since you're interested. Here goes. Right after I graduated from high school, I joined the U.S. Army. You know? See the world. Have an adventure. I did a tour in Afghanistan."

"See the world. Have an adventure. And get shot at?"

"Yeah. In my case, it wasn't shot *at*. It was just plain old shot. I was wounded pretty badly and sent home. I ended up back on the rez at my parents' place so I could recuperate fully."

"Then what happened?"

"You're good at interrogation, you know?" He grinned.

Dylan chuckled. "Thank you. That's a compliment coming from a Special Agent."

Cass chuckled. "Okay. So I got better. I worked at my parents' place and enrolled in the local community college. When I finished there, I moved to Flagstaff and finished a bachelor's degree at Northern Arizona University. The GI Bill paid for my education. Then I joined the Shadow Wolves. After a few years there, and getting shot again, this time by smugglers, I joined the FBI."

"Oh, my god! You were a Shadow Wolf! They are so amazing! I read that they are a special Homeland Security unit, all Native Americans, and they are brilliant trackers. They can find everything and everybody in the desert."

"We're pretty good at tracking, but I wouldn't say we can find *everything* and *everybody*."

"I'm impressed. So you got shot again and decided to move to the FBI where life would be easier?" She laughed and shook her head.

"Something like that." Cass found Dylan's questions very amusing.

"Have you been shot while in the FBI?"

"Not yet." He grinned. "Enough about me. Your turn. Tell me why you moved from Kentucky to Arizona, and why you went from tattoo artist to accountant."

"I'll condense this down. Because they were aging, my parents decided to give up the horse farm and stables. They passed it onto my brother, and they moved into town. He's supposed to pay me a share of the farm's earnings on a regular basis as my part of the inheritance. But he has a wife and four kids, and it costs a lot to run the place. So I never see much coming from him. I had to find a way of making a living."

"Why a tattoo artist?"

"I made a big mistake. It's a long story."

Cass nodded. "Okay. Save it for later."

"I have more questions for you."

"Shoot."

"I don't want to shoot you." She grinned.

He shook his head and chuckled. "Okay. Ask me another question."

"How tall are you?"

"Six three."

"Are you married or do you have a girlfriend?"

He grinned. "Nope."

"Last question. Would you like to go horseback riding with me sometime?"

"I would like that very much." He was surprised at how pleased he felt in that moment.

Dylan stood up. "Okay. I'm going in now."

"Yes. You're a very good interrogator." Cass could hear her laughing as she walked away.

2. Shot Again

Morning. Cass Cosay was up early again, just as he had been every day this week. He loved early morning, especially those precious moments just before the sun appeared over the Rincon Mountains in the eastern sky when everything was waking up. Or going to bed. He saw a couple of coyotes across the street trotting by, focused on their goal. They looked like they were headed to their resting place for the day. Hunt at night. Sleep during the day. The song dog's life.

He liked the evenings, especially when lovely young women interrogated him about his life. He laughed softly at the memory of Dylan Scott approaching him on Sunday after the potluck dinner. And she wasn't shy about asking questions. Much to his surprise, he'd been willing to answer. He didn't usually share much about his life. And what she told him about herself was very interesting. He wondered if she'd ever visited the Fort Apache reservation. He was quite certain that she would really enjoy horseback riding on the reservation's many trails.

After a quick cup of coffee, he put on some cut off blue jeans and an old t-shirt and went jogging. He enjoyed a trip around the Iron Horse neighborhood on his run. Most of the houses were older and on small lots, and there was a small park and community garden on the southern border. He was discovering a few businesses, including a small grocery market, that were scattered throughout the neighborhood. The Iron Horse neighborhood was just east of very busy Fourth Avenue, which provided Tucsonans and visitors easy access to restaurants, bars, night clubs, and businesses of all sorts, including drug dealers who regularly and surreptitiously sought potential buyers. At least some of them were out of business now that he and his team had taken them down about five days ago. Busted and in jail. That's where they belonged.

After the bust, Cass decided to take a couple of weeks off. He wanted to think about things. About his life. He'd been an FBI Special Agent for several years, and a Shadow Wolf before that. He was thinking maybe it was time for a change. Or not. He had a good career with the FBI. The work was interesting, if dangerous at times. But did he want to do it forever? He couldn't say. Sometimes he really missed the reservation. His dad had passed on now, but his mother and siblings all lived there. He missed the quiet of the rez and the beauty of the landscape. He missed the horses. That was something he and Dylan agreed about – the horses. Maybe it was time to go home for a visit.

Back at the apartment, Cass showered and ate a quick breakfast. He settled down in a comfortable chair in front of the big window facing the south. He had a good science-fiction book to read, and he could watch a film on the television, if he felt like it. Later, he'd take a long walk. But mainly, he just wanted to take time to think about his life and what he wanted next. Logan Reid, the apartment manager, came to mind. Cass was a little jealous of Logan because he was a father. Cass had always wanted a kid, or more than one, but he could see it was really challenging, especially because Logan was a single father. Charlie was an adorable handful. Nope, not easy. Cass figured he was better off finding a good woman to share those child-rearing duties. Was he ready for that? Ready for marriage and parenting? He wasn't sure.

And where exactly does one find a "good woman?" He had only been in love, really in love, once in his life. She was a fellow soldier, but she was discharged a few months before him, and she went home. They drifted apart because it was just too difficult to maintain a long distance relationship over several months and from opposite sides of the world. The last time he heard from her, she was marrying some other man. Since then, his interactions with women mostly had not been all that satisfying. Nothing serious. It was that way for the women as well. Just fun and some physical, meaning sexual, affection. Not real love. He hadn't found the right woman. Cass sighed and opened his book.

The day went by slowly. Cass called his mom and had a nice conversation with her. He took a nap. He baked some bread. He read some more. He watched the news on the television. He realized that it was a little after five, and because of that, there was a chance that he might see Dylan returning home. He liked seeing the sun on her dark red hair. "Auburn" was the term. The accounting firm where she worked was on Fourth Avenue not far away, and several times, he'd seen her returning home on foot in the late afternoon. He thought if he saw her today maybe he could ask her when she wanted to go riding.

Yes, there she was. Dylan was moving at a steady pace along the sidewalk and coming closer and closer to Casa Pacifica. She was dressed in a dark blue business suit, and she was carrying her dress shoes in her hand. She had canvas shoes on her feet, a purse was hanging from her shoulder, and her hair was pinned up. Very attractive woman. Cass stood up.

Suddenly a small car pulled up to the curb and stopped right next to Dylan. Three young men got out. They looked to be maybe early or mid-twenties. Dylan had stopped, but not for long. When she attempted to walk quickly away, one of the young men reached out and grabbed her. Or, more accurately, he grabbed one of her breasts really roughly. Cass was on his feet now, headed for the door. By the time he got down the stairs, he could see through the glass that the other two men had trapped Dylan between them. They were lifting her up off her feet, and the one who had grabbed her breasts was now running his hand up her skirt. All three of them were laughing and carrying her toward their car.

Cass knew exactly what they were up to. They were going to abduct her, take her some place quiet and out of the way, and each of them would have a go at her in the backseat of their car. Then they would dump her out on the street and drive away. Bastards. By the time he shoved open the downstairs door and ran toward them, one of them had torn open her blouse and was trying to pull away her bra to expose her breasts. Dylan was kicking and struggling, and when she attempted to scream, one of them punched her face.

"Hey!" Cass yelled. "Let her go!"

The three young men froze for a moment, staring at Cass. One of them looked intently at him and growled. "We know you, *pendejo*. You took down our amigos last week and ruined our sales. We lost a lot of money because of you." He pulled a small pistol from his belt and pointed it at Cass.

"No!" Dylan cried out. She struggled against the men who held her….

About the Author

C.J. Shane is an artist and writer based in Tucson, Arizona, USA. She is author of the Letty Valdez Mystery series, the Cat Miranda Mystery series, the Iron Horse Mystery series, and additional fiction and nonfiction books.